PRAISE FOR

# *MURDER UNDER BLUE SKIES*

"This cozy series kickoff . . . reads like a story told from a front-porch rocker."
—*Publishers Weekly*

"Just the sort of mild, sunny whodunit you'd expect from celebrity weatherman Scott."
—*Kirkus Reviews*

"Stanley and his three pussycats are up to their tails in murder as the book rains down heavy weather lore."
—*New York Post*

"[Willard Scott] has created a homespun, bumbling detective with plenty of charm."
—*Dallas Morning News*

# Murder Under Blue Skies

Willard Scott

*with Bill Crider*

AN ONYX BOOK

ONYX
Published by the Penguin Group
Penguin Putnam Inc., 375 Hudson Street,
New York, New York 10014, U.S.A.
Penguin Books Ltd, 27 Wrights Lane,
London W8 5TZ, England
Penguin Books Australia Ltd, Ringwood,
Victoria, Australia
Penguin Books Canada Ltd, 10 Alcorn Avenue,
Toronto, Ontario, Canada M4V 3B2
Penguin Books (N.Z.) Ltd, 182–190 Wairau Road,
Auckland 10, New Zealand

Penguin Books Ltd, Registered Offices:
Harmondsworth, Middlesex, England

Published by Onyx, an imprint of Dutton NAL,
a member of Penguin Putnam Inc.
Previously appeared in a Dutton edition.

First Onyx Printing, January, 1999
10 9 8 7 6 5 4 3 2 1

Printed in the United States of America



PUBLISHER'S NOTE
This is a work of fiction. Names, characters, places, and incidents either are the products of the author's imagination or are used fictitiously, and any resemblance to actual persons, living or dead, events, or locales is entirely coincidental.

## AUTHOR'S NOTE

Readers of the following pages who suspect that the author has considerably fiddled with the geography of Virginia are absolutely correct. The town of Higgins is not to be found on any map; the town, its inhabitants, and the surrounding countryside are strictly products of the author's imagination. The author hereby tenders his apologies to any communities that have been squeezed out of his version of Virginia to make room for Higgins and its fictional environs.

## AUTHOR'S DISCLAIMER

For thousands of years, everybody's been talking about the weather. As a result, we have hundreds of folk sayings that tell us when to plant crops, when we can expect rain, and when we're going to have a hard winter. However, what Benjamin Franklin said about people can also apply to these folk sayings: "Some are weatherwise. Some are otherwise."

So I'm not making any claims that all the sayings collected in this book are true. On the other hand, I'm not saying that they're totally inaccurate. After all, they're based on observations that must at some time or other have seemed entirely valid to someone, and they wouldn't have survived for as long as they have if people at some time and place hadn't found a certain amount of truth to them. My father, for example, didn't have a barometer, but he believed that when smoke came down the chimney instead of rising up it, snow was sure to fall. And you know what? Every now and then, he was right.

That doesn't mean that you'll be able to get a job replacing your local TV weather forecaster just by memorizing the bits of wisdom scattered throughout this book. But you'll probably be right at least part of the time—just like he is.

# 1

# Salsa Dip

Everything was going wonderfully well at the gala grand opening of the Blue Skies Bed & Breakfast Inn, right up until the moment Belinda Grimsby collapsed facedown into a bowl of homemade salsa.

"Damn," said Stanley Waters, though he might be forgiven the mild expletive, considering that it was not the worst he had ever uttered. And, after all, he had put several months into planning his grand opening party for the day before the arrival of the first guests. He had truly wanted it to be a success. The guys from the network were there with their cameras, recording everything, and shots of a woman diving headfirst into the salsa were a long way from the kind of publicity that Stanley, as a fledgling innkeeper, had hoped to gain through his first big promotion.

"Ol' bat probably did it on purpose if I know her," Bill Caldwell said as he and Stanley made their way through the crowd toward the inquisitive onlookers who had gathered around the table beside which Belinda was lying.

Bill was the inn's housekeeper, a tall, rangy man with watery blue eyes whom Stanley had hired mainly because of his wife, Caroline. Caroline was without question the best cook in Higgins, Virginia, or maybe the entire state, and she had insisted that she and Bill were a package deal. Stanley's theory was that food was the basis of any successful bed-and-breakfast, so he bought the package.

"She's been jealous of Caroline for years," Bill went on. "Truth to tell, she's never been the same since Caroline won the blue ribbon for her chocolate pie back in their home ec class at Higgins High."

Stanley wasn't interested in ancient feuds. What really bothered him was that Belinda had toppled over during an incredibly lively bluegrass rendition of "Blue Moon of Kentucky" by Little Melvin and the Moonshiners. She had, in fact, taken her fall right in the middle of a complex mandolin solo, causing the TV cameras to turn directly from Little Melvin to her, a detail that was sure to displease Little Melvin, who had emphasized to Stanley that he was cutting his usual performance fee not because he was a friend of Stanley's but because he needed the free publicity he'd get on *Hello, World!*

To tell the truth, nearly all the paid participants in the day's events had taken a cut because Stanley had practically guaranteed their appearance on his former TV show, the number one–rated morning program in the world. Stanley was sure Sam Foley, the show's producer, would go along, and he'd been right. Now Stanley wasn't sure it had been such a good idea.

Up until Belinda's untimely topple into the salsa, things had been proceeding according to plan. The weather, as Stanley had predicted in a guest shot on *Hello, World!* only about fifteen minutes earlier, was perfect. The temperature hovered near seventy degrees, and the sky was such a brilliant blue that it hurt Stanley's eyes to look at it.

A group of amateur cloggers had started off the morning's festivities on the stage that Hal Tipton, the inn's handyman, had built to Stanley's precise specifications. The cloggers' feet had pounded the stage until it had throbbed as if with the sound of distant thunder, and the applause had been even more thunderous.

The cloggers had been followed by the local square dance club, all flouncing petticoats and calico shirts, and the square dance club had been followed by a very good local magician, who could not only pull rabbits out of his own hat but out of the hats of the male square dancers.

The magician had been followed in turn by Little Melvin and his bluegrass group, a group that had slowly been building a national following in spite of country radio's preference for blandly sentimental tunes sung by good-looking young men in huge Western hats.

Not only had the crowd appreciated each successive act, but the sound system had responded perfectly to Little Melvin—no reverb or feedback, just the clear, precise tones of mandolin, fiddle, guitar, and Little Melvin's crystalline tenor.

And the TV crew had been getting all of it live for *Hello, World!*'s nationwide audience. The publicity (free, of course) would have been enough to get the inn off to a roaring start, but now Stanley was sure that the only thing people would remember was the shot of Belinda Grimsby's head being pulled out of the salsa bowl, little bits of fresh tomato clinging to her graying hair and spicy liquid dripping off her chin.

By the time he and Bill reached the table, Belinda was stretched out on the ground beside it and Jimmy Nugent was applying CPR. Stanley had hired Jimmy's firm to provide security for the day's festivities, and it appeared that Jimmy was ready for any emergency.

"Excuse me," Stanley said, pushing his way through the crowd as politely as he could.

More and more people were gathering around as word of the incident spread, and Stanley was beginning to regret ever having decided to go into innkeeping. Maybe he should have stuck with television.

As the word about Belinda's mishap spread, people came toward the food tables from all over the grounds, leaving the fortune-telling booth, deserting the auto show provided by a local dealer, ignoring the attractions of the free tour of the inn's restored interior. Little Melvin and his group were trying to get people's attention with a spirited version of "Rocky Top," but it wasn't working. Everyone seemed fascinated by the woman on the ground and the man who straddled her, pumping on her chest.

Two or three people, however, weren't watching Jimmy. They were talking into cellular telephones. Stanley was sure they were notifying any newspaper and TV stations not already covering the event, but he realized that he was being less than charitable when he heard the sirens. The phone callers had all dialed 911, and the ambulance was on its way.

Stanley didn't wait for its arrival. A large man, he was able to shove forward to the small cleared area near Belinda and Jimmy. A TV cameraman whom Stanley didn't know was right there, getting close-ups of Jimmy as he tried to force air into Belinda's lungs.

"What happened, Jimmy?" Stanley asked, kneeling on the freshly clipped grass beside Belinda, who didn't look good at all. "Did she swallow a jalapeño?"

"Worse than that," Jimmy said.

"Worse than swallowing a jalapeño?"

Jimmy didn't answer. He had to pause to breathe into Belinda's mouth. When he was done, he started pumping on her chest again.

"What's worse than swallowing a jalapeño?" Stanley asked, not at all sure that he wanted to hear the answer.

"Being dead," Jimmy said without turning to look at Stanley. "That's worse."

"Damn," Stanley said again.

# 2

# Live TV

Stanley looked up at the curious faces surrounding him, wondering if anyone had heard Nugent's comment. Everyone he saw was familiar to him. He'd met all of them, and he'd done business with most of them since moving to Higgins to start Blue Skies.

Barry Miller, who looked like a 1950s matinee idol grown old and distinguished, his silver hair swept back from his face in wings, was whispering in the ear of his partner, Tommy Bright, whose face had lost its perpetual smile. The two of them owned M & B Antiques, a store just off the town square, and Stanley had bought some of his furnishings from them. They had given him a slight discount because of his fame, but not enough to keep the costs from being within the range of what Stanley considered exorbitant.

Lacy Falk was a big woman with big hair. Her styling salon was the center of town gossip, and she was excitedly talking to Ellen Winston, who managed the General Lee Hotel, located across the street from City Hall. Ellen's purse dangled from her arm as she twisted her hands. She seemed about to burst into tears. She was Belinda's best friend, and she had regarded Stanley as unwanted competition from the minute his plans to open Blue Skies were announced. He knew that she would cheerfully inform every tourist under her roof of what had happened.

And then there was that cameraman.

"Why don't you turn around and give the viewers some shots of Little Melvin and the boys," Stanley suggested. " 'Rocky Top' is one of their best numbers."

The cameraman just grinned. He knew what the TV audience wanted to see, and women who fell into a bowl of salsa and required CPR were a lot more interesting to most people than a semi-obscure bluegrass combo, even if the combo seemed to be on the verge of breaking out nationally.

Hal Tipton bent down, looking concerned. He was a single man who had from time to time dated Belinda, though that did not make him unique. Belinda was perhaps the most-often-engaged, never-married woman in Virginia.

"Is she gonna be all right, Stanley?" Hal asked, as if he were the only person in the crowd who hadn't heard Nugent's words.

"I don't know," Stanley said. "Maybe."

Hey, it wasn't a lie. Who was Stanley to say what might happen to Belinda? He could hope for the best, couldn't he? After all, he wasn't a doctor, and neither was Nugent. Maybe Belinda would be just fine, though it certainly didn't seem likely. Her face and lips were an ashy gray, and she looked as lifeless as a lug wrench.

"She was really gobbling that salsa," Corey Gainer said.

Gainer managed the Palace Theater, an old movie palace that had been refurbished but only slightly modernized. Stanley had been to only one movie there since returning to Higgins, and the film had broken at a crucial juncture. Gainer hadn't been able to get things fixed, and Stanley had gotten a refund.

"Salsa's good for you," Hal said. "No fat, and it has peppers in it. Peppers have something in them that's supposed to be good for heart disease."

"Didn't do Belinda much good," Gainer said.

Stanley wasn't pleased with the direction the

conversation was taking. He wished the EMS crew would hurry up and get there, and as if in response to his wish he heard someone saying, "Make way. Give us a little room."

Two men in white pushed through the crowd and set a stretcher down beside Belinda.

"How about it, Jim?" one of the men asked.

"I'm afraid she's gone," Nugent said. "But maybe you guys can help."

"What happened?" the man asked.

"It was the salsa," Corey Gainer said. "I bet she choked on it."

Stanley stood up and looked at the table. It was covered with a white cloth, and on the cloth were several bowls of salsa with baked chips beside them. The table also held tomatoes, yellow squash sliced into circles, cauliflower, and broccoli. The tomatoes had come from Stanley's own garden, out behind Blue Skies. Besides the vegetables, there were breadsticks and fruit: apple slices, pineapple chunks, melon balls. Stanley was watching his weight, and he'd wanted his guests to enjoy healthy, low-fat snacks.

Stanley got to his feet. "The salsa didn't hurt her," he said.

"Darn right it didn't," Bill Caldwell said. "My wife made it up fresh in the kitchen, and everything she makes is the best there is. Everybody knows that."

There were murmurs of agreement from the crowd. Caroline Caldwell's reputation as a cook had long ago spread throughout Higgins. Her biscuits were so light that they seemed to hover above the plate, and her chocolate pies had been known to send even the most dour individuals into eye-rolling ecstasy.

"Belinda wouldn't agree with that," Lacy Falk said. "Belinda said more than once that Caroline's cooking was highly overrated."

"That's because Belinda couldn't ever beat her even when they were in home ec," Bill said. "And after that, she couldn't beat her at the county fair. Caroline won every blue ribbon she ever tried for. Belinda never got better than third, so anything she said was just sour grapes."

Belinda didn't look to Stanley as if she'd ever win third again. The EMS men had put her onto the stretcher and popped it up. Stanley watched as they pushed her through the crowd toward the waiting ambulance.

When they reached the ambulance, they put Belinda inside, closed the doors, and took off, siren wailing. The cameraman got a good shot of the departing vehicle, and then the thing Stanley had been dreading happened. Nancy Holden was heading for him, holding a microphone. She was *Hello, World!*'s human-interest reporter, and she'd been walking around the grounds, followed by yet another cameraman, doing brief interviews with some of the attendees, and now she was after Stanley.

He took Jim Nugent's arm and tried to pull him away, hoping to lose Nancy in the crowd that was beginning to disperse and pay more attention to the Moonshiners now that all the excitement was over.

Jim didn't move. His voice was a husky croak. "She's gone, Stanley. I tried, but I couldn't save her."

Stanley patted Jim Nugent on the back. "You did what you could, Jim. I appreciate it, and I'm sure Belinda does, too. She'll pull through."

Nugent shook his head. "No, she won't. I never saw anything like it. I was standing right over there." He pointed to a spot not far from the table. "She was eating a little of everything, but the salsa was what she really liked. I guess a lot of people these days are eating that stuff."

Stanley nodded and glanced apprehensively at Nancy Holden, who'd stopped to talk to a woman holding a small girl by the hand. Maybe she'd be distracted.

"Salsa's supposedly more popular than ketchup," he told Nugent. "People eat it on everything."

"I never liked it much, myself," Nugent said. "Too hot. I don't like hot things."

Nugent was about Stanley's age, but he was much thinner, and he had a full head of dark, thick hair. Stanley lifted his BLUE SKIES INN cap and ran his hand over his bare scalp, trying to remember how long it had been since he'd had enough hair to cover his head. Too long, not that Stanley cared. Many women found bald men attractive. At least that's what Stanley had heard. He hadn't found much evidence of it lately.

"Belinda liked the salsa, though," Stanley said, hoping to bring Nugent back to the topic.

"She sure did. But then something happened."

"What?"

Nugent got a melancholy look in his eyes, as if he were seeing it happen again. "Her face started twitching. Like she was trying to get a fly off her nose or something. And then she started quivering all over like ants were stinging her. That's when I started toward her. But by the time I got to the table, her face was already in the salsa. I guess I pulled her out before she could drown."

That reminded Stanley of something. He looked back toward the table, where Bill Caldwell was removing the bowl of salsa into which Belinda had taken a header.

Good, Stanley thought. Wouldn't want anyone dipping into salsa flavored by Belinda's makeup.

He started to turn back to Nugent, and that was when he saw Marilyn Tunney.

Nugent saw her at the same time and said, "Uh-oh."

That pretty much summed up Stanley's feelings as well. Things had been bad enough before, and now they were going to get worse.

Although Nugent was wearing a uniform, he wasn't a certified officer.

Marilyn Tunney was. Now the real cops had arrived.

# 3

# Old Friends

Marilyn Tunney had, in a sense, inherited the job as chief of police for Higgins, Virginia. Her husband had been the chief for nearly twenty years, until he had died of a heart attack suffered in the line of duty while rescuing a dog that had gotten itself stuck in a storm drain. The dog, as far as Stanley knew, was still alive and doing fine.

At the time of her husband's death, Marilyn had been a detective on the force. It seemed logical to the members of the Higgins City Council for her to step into the chief's job, and she had accepted their offer.

Stanley had known her for most of his life. They had begun elementary school together at the age of six in a tottering old brick building that no longer existed. It had been torn down and replaced by a brick and steel structure that didn't even have windows. Stanley thought it looked more like a prison than a school building. Every time he saw it, he was glad that his school days were long behind him.

Stanley and Marilyn had been good friends for most of their time in the Higgins school system, and they had even dated for two years during high school. Stanley had been serious about the romance, but after graduation they had drifted apart, Stanley to the Northeast to pursue the radio career that eventually led him into television, and Marilyn to Richmond to attend college.

They had met at high school reunions over the years, and Stanley had always been amazed at how Marilyn didn't seem to change. As Stanley's hair began to thin and his waistline to expand, she remained the same petite, dark-haired, blue-eyed woman that he remembered from 1958. There was a little gray in the hair now, but not much. Stanley wondered if Lacy knew the secret of that, or if there was one.

He moved over to get between Marilyn and Nancy Holden, still preoccupied by the woman and child, but he was shoved aside by Officer Mike Kunkel, in full uniform and full of authority, as usual.

Kunkel was as big as Stanley, but much better

equipped. He had everything except a wrist radio, but then he didn't need one. He had a microphone clipped to his right epaulet instead, and his middle was surrounded by a utility belt that Batman would envy. The radio receiver was there, and in addition the belt's shiny leather compartments held silver handcuffs; pepper Mace; a dark, hard-looking, highly polished baton; and two clips of spare ammo for the automatic pistol that was clasped in a holster riding high on Kunkel's right hip. Stanley didn't much like pistols.

For that matter, he didn't much like Kunkel, either.

"Back off, Waters," Kunkel said. "You're impeding a police investigation."

Stanley was a little surprised that Kunkel knew a word like *impeding*, but it was the word *investigation* that made Nancy Holden look up, as alert as a pointer nearing a covey of quail. The little girl to whom Nancy had been talking, while cute and engaging enough, couldn't compete with an investigation of any kind.

"What investigation?" Stanley asked, wishing the kid would trip Nancy with the mike cord or maybe grab the mike from her hand and stick it in a pitcher of lemonade.

"*This* investigation," Marilyn said. "I'm sorry,

Stanley, but we have to look into what happened to Belinda." She turned to the table. "Don't go anywhere with that bowl, Bill."

Bill Caldwell was already several yards away, but he turned around when Marilyn called his name.

"Me?" he said.

"You," Marilyn said. "We'll have to see that the contents of that bowl are analyzed."

Stanley stared at her. "Analyzed?"

"To see if that stuff's been poisoned," Marilyn said, turning back to him. "From what I've heard, it's an obvious possibility."

Nancy, timing it perfectly, arrived just at that moment.

"And what possibility is that, Officer?" she asked, thrusting the microphone in Kunkel's face.

Kunkel looked at Nancy, then at the cameraman, then at Chief Tunney. He clearly wanted to say something, but he didn't want to say anything that his boss wouldn't approve of.

"I'll have to let the chief answer that," Kunkel said finally.

Then Nancy made a big mistake. Stanley knew it was a mistake as soon as the words were out of Nancy's mouth, and he allowed himself a small smile.

"And where is the chief?" Nancy asked.

Because she was the chief, Marilyn had the luxury of wearing street clothes, and Stanley had to admit that she didn't really look much like the stereotypical small-town flatfoot in her navy blue slacks and matching jacket. She didn't look like a cop of any kind. She was only about five feet four inches tall, and she wasn't wearing a badge or carrying a gun. She didn't have a utility belt, either.

On the other hand, Stanley thought, Nancy should have known better than to let stereotypes affect her judgment.

Except that Nancy, who was quite attractive in a horsey way, and pretty good at asking innocuous questions of mothers and their little daughters, wasn't exactly at her best while trying actual journalism.

And so she made another mistake, even bigger than the first one. After glancing around for a second, she stuck the mike under Jim Nugent's nose.

"Tell me, Chief," she said, "just exactly what kind of investigation is being conducted here?"

It was all Stanley could do to keep a straight face. Nugent, while an amiable enough guy, wasn't exactly chief material in Stanley's opinion. True, he was the head of his own security service, and he was wearing a uniform, which Stanley had to admit was even gaudier than Kunkel's. But the uniform lacked certain necessary elements, the most important of which was an official badge.

Nugent reacted as many other people would have done, given the opportunity to appear on national TV and not being hampered by job protocol as Kunkel had been. He took immediate advantage of the situation.

Instead of telling Nancy that he wasn't the chief, he said, "It's a really important investigation, Miss Holden. Is it all right if I call you 'Miss Holden'?"

"Of course, Chief. Now we all saw what happened here—"

That was a lie, Stanley thought. Nancy couldn't have seen much of it. She was off doing her little interviews. But he didn't interrupt.

"—but would you care to give us your take on it?"

"Well," Nugent said, puffing out his chest a little, "what happened was—"

Hal Tipton, standing at Stanley's shoulder, said, "He's no more a police chief than I am. He doesn't know what happened here any more than a goat."

Nancy was a pro. She managed not to look flustered. She cut her eyes to Stanley, who shrugged and said, "He's right. About the chief part, anyway. I don't know about the goat part."

"Then who's the chief?" Nancy mouthed.

Stanley pointed to Marilyn. "She is."

"I see," Nancy said, but it was clear that she didn't. Not quite.

Stanley noted with satisfaction that the camera was turned on Nancy's face, in which at least a bit of her confusion registered.

But once again Nancy's professionalism came into play. She didn't waste time debating with herself about whether Stanley was pulling her leg. She stepped right over to Marilyn and pointed the mike. "Chief, would you care to tell our audience what's going on here?"

Marilyn looked at the red light on the camera. She didn't seem to Stanley to find the situation nearly as appealing as Jim Nugent had. "I'm sorry, but it's a police matter. I can't discuss it."

"But our audience has a right to know."

"That's not true."

"It's not?"

"Of course not. What happened here has nothing at all to do with your audience. Your audience is watching to see the grand opening of the Blue Skies Inn, not to hear me discuss some unfortunate accident."

Stanley felt like hugging her. In fact, the idea

had a lot of appeal on other grounds as well, but Stanley tried not to think about that.

"There are some wonderful things to see here," Marilyn went on. "A magnificent old restored house, for one thing. Little Melvin and the Moonshiners, for another." She waved a hand. "These beautiful grounds, too."

She was laying it on a little thick, but Stanley didn't try to stop her. He was even thinking about asking her if she'd go to work as the inn's PR person. Come to think of it, a PR person wouldn't be a bad idea. But Marilyn probably wouldn't take the job.

"And Stanley has a garden, too," Marilyn said. "Have you seen his garden?"

Stanley was amazed. He'd had no idea that Marilyn knew about the garden. Had she been on a tour of the grounds without telling him? On the other hand, she was a cop. A trained investigator. She probably knew about everything in Higgins, even Stanley's garden.

"I haven't seen the garden," Nancy said.

"Well, you certainly should," Marilyn told her. "It's around in the back of the house. It's really quite a sight. Stanley has a green thumb."

The camera swung around to Stanley, who made a thumbs-up sign. He wished he'd thought to paint his thumb green for the occasion, but he'd had no way of knowing he might get the chance to show it.

"Hal," Stanley said, "why don't you take Nancy to see the garden? You could tell her a little about it on the way."

"Be glad to. I helped out with it a lot," Hal added for Nancy's benefit.

He started walking, and after a second's hesitation, during which she gave Marilyn a searching look, Nancy followed, the cameraman trailing along behind.

"Thanks," Stanley said to Marilyn when the little procession had moved away.

"Just doing my job. I don't like nosy TV people much."

Seeing Stanley's crestfallen look, Marilyn added, "Present company excepted of course. And you aren't nosy, after all. You're just a weatherman."

Stanley's face fell farther.

"I didn't mean that the way it sounded," Marilyn said with a little laugh.

"I hope not." Stanley laughed with her, and he realized that he really meant it. To change the subject he said, "What do you think could be wrong with the food?"

"I hate to say anything before we have it tested."

Kunkel, however, had no such compunctions. "We think it might've been poisoned."

Stanley goggled at him. "What?"

"That's right," Kunkel said. "We think somebody tried to murder that woman. In fact, from the way things look, I'd say somebody did more than just try. Somebody succeeded."

"You're kidding," Stanley said.

Kunkel didn't smile. "I never kid."

Stanley believed him. His face looked harder than a bag of rocks.

"Great way to start a business, huh, boss?" Bill Caldwell said. But he wasn't smiling, either.

# 4

# Dreaming of Blue Skies

Stanley Waters had come to Virginia to run an inn, not to get involved in murder.

Blue Skies had been a dream of his for quite a while, ever since his wife, Jane, had died after a long and debilitating bout with breast cancer. Jane had always been the one who kept him going through the ups and downs of his career, and she suffered just as much as he through every setback, not that there had been too many of those. She had also taken just as much pleasure as he did out of each success.

It hadn't always been easy. He'd met her while he was working for a little radio station in Rhode Island ("That's the only kind of radio stations they have there," he often said afterward; corny maybe, but it usually got a laugh), and they'd married after a courtship of only a few weeks.

Neither of them had ever had any regrets, not even during the early years when Stanley was doing farm shows at five in the morning. Or at least Stanley didn't have any regrets, and he was pretty sure Jane hadn't either.

When she died, it was as if some essential part of him had been amputated. Nothing he did after that seemed to mean very much.

He was one of the most recognized personalities in America, "the weathermeister," as he was known to the audience of *Hello, World!* He was the man who didn't know how to frown, and his open smile made him popular with everyone from kids in kindergarten to centenarians in retirement homes. He'd done more supermarket openings than Coca-Cola, visited more hospitals than the stork. If you stopped ten people on the street and showed his photo side by side with a photo of the president of the United States, only six of those ten people could name the president. Seven could name Stanley.

It had been an exciting and stimulating life, and Stanley had loved every minute of it for as long as Jane had been there to share it with him. But after Jane's death, it suddenly hadn't been fun anymore, and for the first time he learned how to frown. When that happened, he knew that it was time to try something else.

It hadn't been easy to convince his coworkers, especially the *Hello, World!* anchors, who depended on Stanley for a lighthearted quip when things bogged down or when a guest seemed intent on dragging the pace of the show to a halt.

And it hadn't been easy to convince the network brass, who knew that a lot of people watched the show every single day for no other reason than that Stanley did the hourly weather updates and occasionally bantered with the anchors and the guests.

It wasn't that his forecasting was any more accurate than that of any other forecaster; the truth was that Stanley didn't do his own forecasting. He got the reports directly from the weather bureau and gave them out almost exactly as he received them, a fact that he cheerfully and frequently admitted on the air.

That might have been what people liked: a weatherman who didn't pretend to know much more about what the weather was going to do than they did themselves. Whatever it was, the audience liked him a lot, and they didn't want him to leave, either.

But he'd made up his mind, and six months

after his wife's death, he'd begun reducing his workload. For a while he appeared for four days a week, then three. Within two years, he was down to an occasional guest shot, and Blue Skies was on the way to becoming a reality.

He'd decided on Higgins because he'd grown up there, and he'd decided on an inn because he'd always liked meeting new people and making them smile and feel good. He liked seeing them enjoy themselves, whether at a good meal or just relaxing in comfortable surroundings. He liked gardening, and he liked small towns and the people who lived in them. He liked the old ways of doing things, the ways he'd grown up with and still believed in.

What better way to combine all the things he liked than by becoming an innkeeper in a small Virginia town? It had been a tremendous stroke of luck to find a suitable place in Higgins, where he had grown up. Or so he had thought until a few minutes ago, when Belinda Grimsby had tumbled into the salsa.

It had been bad enough when it seemed like an accident.

It was sounding a lot worse now.

"What makes you think someone killed her?" he asked Marilyn.

"I was monitoring the 911 calls," she said. "One of the callers described what was happening, and it sounded like poisoning was a definite possibility."

Stanley thought about what Jim Nugent had said, and he looked at the security man.

Nugent nodded. "Looked that way to me, too, Stanley. It's something you have to consider when something like this happens, no matter how small you think the chances are."

"It could have been something else," Marilyn said. "A stroke, maybe, or a heart attack. But we have to be certain."

"But who'd want to kill Belinda?" Stanley couldn't imagine such a thing.

"Maybe no one," Marilyn said. "We don't know that anyone killed her. We don't want to jump to any conclusions."

"Seems like you're jumping to me," Bill Caldwell said.

Bill was standing by Marilyn with the bowl of salsa in his hands. He was looking down at it as if a black widow spider might be swimming around under the chunky surface.

"We haven't reached any conclusions, by jumping or by other means," Marilyn told him. "We're just going to check things out. That's all."

Bill continued to study the salsa. If there was a

spider, it wasn't moving. "How could poison get in there?"

"That's an easy one," Kunkel said. "Somebody put it in there."

"If it's in there at all," Marilyn added.

Kunkel took the bowl from Bill's hands. "If there is, the lab'll find out." Kunkel glanced over at the table. "And I'd say we'd better take the rest of that food, too."

Stanley shrugged. "Why not?"

It really wouldn't matter. There wasn't anyone at the table now, anyhow. It was as if Belinda's death had put people off their feed, not that Stanley could blame them if they were no longer in the mood to eat. The food just didn't look as appetizing as it had earlier, somehow. The melon balls didn't look quite as red, the cauliflower looked speckled. The broccoli looked floppy as a nag's ear.

"I'll be back," Kunkel said, then marched off with the salsa.

"Arnold Schwarzenegger, *The Terminator*," Hal said, joining them.

"I thought you were showing Nancy the garden," Stanley said.

"I showed it to her. She's not big on gardens, though."

"Kunkel doesn't have the muscles to be Arnold Schwarzenegger," Bill said.

Hal nodded. "Got the mouth, though."

Stanley raised a hand. "Let's not be disrespectful of the police. They're just doing their job."

"Maybe," Bill said, watching Kunkel's retreating back. "I never thought much of that one, though."

"He's a good officer," Marilyn said. "Most of the time, anyway."

"Do you want us to help you carry any of the food?" Stanley asked.

Marilyn shook her head. "No, thanks."

"I don't think she trusts us," Hal said. "She's afraid we might 'accidentally' drop something on the ground and destroy the evidence."

Marilyn gave him a straight look. "Hal Tipton, how long have you known me?"

Hal thought for a second. "Probably since you were about ten years old. I used to do the occasional odd job for your daddy back in those days. Sometimes you'd even help me out."

Hal had spent most of his life doing odd jobs, which was the reason Stanley had hired him to work at Blue Skies. Hal loved to mow lawns, he understood the intricacies of electrical wiring, he could fix small engines and motors, and he didn't mind working with the inn's sometimes cranky plumbing.

"So you've known me for forty years or so," Marilyn said.

"More or less."

"And you think I don't trust you."

Hal grinned. "That's right. You're too smart for that. If any of that food's really poisoned, then it was somebody here that poisoned it. And we're here."

"Wait a minute," Stanley said. "Does that mean she doesn't trust me, either?"

"What about me?" Bill asked.

"She'd be a damn fool to trust a single one of us," Hal said. "And if there's one thing she's not, it's a damn fool. Right, Chief?"

Marilyn smiled at him. "You've known me a long time, all right, Hal. But you don't understand me as well as you think you do. I trust you. And you, too, Stanley. And Bill. But in the police business we have what's called a chain of custody. If we let someone else handle the evidence, the chain's broken. Defense lawyers love that kind of thing. Cops don't."

"Still boils down to the fact that you don't trust us," Hal said.

But Stanley didn't see it that way. He thought he

understood what Marilyn was getting at, and he appreciated her professionalism.

"What about the rest of the food?" he asked. "Caroline's fixing up a lot more."

"I'd suggest you save her the trouble," Marilyn said. "Let everyone enjoy the music and the entertainment, and forget about the food."

"I was afraid you'd say that."

"See what I mean?" Hal said. "She doesn't trust us."

"How long before you get the lab report?" Stanley asked.

"A few days. We don't have our own lab. We'll have to send it to Alexandria."

Higgins wasn't exactly remote, but it was several miles from any city of significant size. Alexandria was the nearest.

"You could always send it to Langley and let the CIA have a look," Hal suggested.

"I don't think that will be necessary," Marilyn told him. "This isn't exactly a matter of international security."

"Never can tell," Hal said. "Might be folks keeling over in Iraq right this very minute."

"Hal," Stanley said, "why don't you go over and listen to Little Melvin? You said you really liked that bluegrass music."

Hal started to protest, changed his mind, and walked away toward the stage where the Moonshiners were soaring through an instrumental. Stanley thought it was "Foggy Mountain Breakdown."

"I don't know what got into Hal," Stanley said. "He's usually not like that at all."

"Sudden death affects people in different ways," Marilyn said. "It's nothing to worry about."

Stanley was worried anyway, and it wasn't just Hal's behavior that was bothering him. "You'll let us know about what really happened to Belinda, won't you?"

"That's another thing you don't have to worry about," Marilyn said. "One way or another, I'll let you know."

The words sounded harmless enough. Stanley wondered why they seemed so ominous.

# 5

# Hair Today, Gone Tomorrow

People were distracted from Belinda's unfortunate collapse soon enough, thanks to all the other attractions around them, and Stanley didn't tell any of his visitors about the phone call he got from Marilyn a bit later to tell him that Belinda had been dead before she was put into the ambulance.

Stanley and Belinda had never been friends, and she didn't have any family left that he knew about. Probably not too many residents of Higgins would mourn her passing, but Stanley was depressed and sad all the same. It just didn't seem right for someone who appeared to be so healthy one minute to be dead the next. And it certainly didn't seem right that she could have been murdered.

The more Stanley thought about it, however, the more certain he was that murder was out of the question. True, Belinda didn't have a great many friends in Higgins, but surely there was no one who would want to kill her. She must have died from natural causes, probably a heart attack, though some would say that Belinda didn't *have* a heart.

Stanley tried to put her death out of his mind and enjoy the festivities, but he found that it just wasn't possible. No matter what he was doing, the thought of Belinda lurked at the back of his mind like a nagging doubt.

Fortunately, the rest of the day passed more or less uneventfully, unless you counted the middle-aged man and woman that an eleven-year-old boy and his mother caught skinny-dipping down at the creek that wound through the trees at the back of the inn's property.

"They said they couldn't resist," Jim Nugent told Stanley. "They said the atmosphere was just so perfect that it reminded them of when they were kids."

Stanley didn't suppose it mattered much if the couple had been caught. He'd been hoping that people would feel at home at Blue Skies. Apparently they would. Maybe they were going to feel a little too much at home.

Stanley and Nugent were sitting on the porch of the inn in two of the four Kennedy rockers lined up along the wall of the old house. Stanley was rocking, but Nugent had his feet propped up on the railing.

Stanley liked the porch. He liked to sit there in the late afternoon and look out over the grounds as he was doing now. The open area in front of the inn was a little the worse for wear after the day's events, but Bill and Hal had picked up most of the trash, and the only thing remaining to be removed was the stage that Hal had built. Stanley was thinking about leaving it for a while. It might be a good idea to have other performances, say on the weekends, to get a bit more publicity. Maybe he could get a few fairly big names to come in and perform cheap. Or give square-dancing lessons. Anything to draw a crowd and get a little free advertising. It was worth a try, anyway.

"The kid's mother wasn't too happy about it," Nugent said, bringing Stanley back to reality. "She says he might be traumatized."

"Does that mean she's going to cause trouble?"

"Nah. The kid blurted out that it was her idea to go down to the creek. She wanted to see if there were any birds in the trees, and she dragged him along. He didn't want to go."

The trees near the creek were full of Virginia warblers and cardinals. Stanley's three cats, who had spent most of their lives cooped up in a city apartment, often sat and stared at the birds as if they'd like to do something about them, but so far they hadn't. At least not as far as Stanley knew. He'd seen no suspicious feathers lying in the grass, and no carcasses had been deposited at the inn's back door.

"Did she see any birds?" Stanley wondered.

Nugent hadn't asked. "Anyway, it was her idea to go down there, and she ignored that yellow warning tape all around. She had to duck under the tape to get to the creek, so she doesn't have much room for complaint."

It had been Nugent's idea to put up the tape, which was printed with black letters reading RESTRICTED AREA, KEEP OUT! every couple of feet. Nugent had been in the security business in Alexandria for several years, and he knew a little about the kinds of things people could get themselves into. The creek, he had warned Stanley, was asking for trouble.

"What about Belinda?" Stanley asked.

"Hard to say about that," Nugent answered. Stanley had told him about her being dead. "It'll all depend on the lab report, and the autopsy. Like Marilyn said, don't worry about it."

"Easy for you to say."

"Right. I don't have the investment that you do." Nugent removed his feet from the railing and stood up. "I guess I'd better get on back to Alexandria. It's been a pleasure working for you, Stanley."

Stanley stood up, too, and they shook hands.

"The pleasure was all mine," Stanley said.

Nugent had given him a discount rate because they'd gone to school together at Higgins High. Nugent had been a year ahead of Stanley and Marilyn.

"That Marilyn's something, isn't she?" Nugent said as he walked down the porch steps.

"You mean she's a good cop?"

"That, too. But I meant that she's still a looker. Mark Tunney was lucky to get her. I always thought she was smarter than he was, and pretty besides. Come to think of it, you used to go out with her, didn't you? I always thought you and she would get together."

"I thought so, too, for a while. But things change, and that was a long time ago."

"Not so long. Sometimes it seems like about a week and a half."

Stanley knew what Nugent meant. The years had a way of sneaking by when you weren't looking.

"I've been thinking about asking her out," Nugent said. "You think she'd go?"

"She'll have to answer that one herself," Stanley said, surprised that Nugent would confide in him.

"Yeah, I guess so. Well, I'll see you, Stanley. You take care, now."

"I will."

Stanley sat back down and watched Nugent walk across the clipped green grass toward his dark blue car. A magnetized metal sign was on the door. Painted in blue letters on the sign's silver badge was J & N SECURITY SERVICES. The J & N stood for James and Nugent, Stanley supposed. He didn't think that Nugent had a partner.

Stanley wondered whether Marilyn would go out with Nugent. He wasn't a bad-looking guy. He was still lean, and he had only one chin. Not to mention all that hair.

Stanley lifted off his BLUE SKIES baseball cap and ran his hand across the top of his head. Still as slick as ever. He'd started losing his hair when he was just a kid, and he'd almost forgotten what it had felt like to run his fingers through it.

He had a pretty nice growth around the sides, though. Maybe he could try a comb-over. No, he thought, if he did that, he'd look like Zero Mostel. And who'd want to rent a room from Zero Mostel?

Besides, what difference did it make if he was bald? Stanley wasn't thinking about asking Marilyn out.

Or was he?

For the first time since Jane's death he found himself thinking about another woman. And not just thinking about her but thinking about how it might be to talk to her over a dinner table or in a car as they were driving along some winding country road.

She probably wasn't interested, however, and if she were, his baldness wouldn't be a hindrance. Marilyn wasn't the kind of person to let something like that bother her.

But Nugent had spoken first. Besides, Stanley had an inn to run. He'd better think about that and put any thoughts of romance out of his head. The inn was opening for business tomorrow, and he'd have his hands full with his first guests. He wouldn't have time for Marilyn. And even if he did have time, he was probably too old for romance.

He smiled. He might *look* too old, at least to the Generation X kids, but for the first time in a couple of years he surely didn't feel that way.

He looked to the west where the sun was setting behind the Blue Ridge. The few cirrus clouds on the horizon were tinged with pink and orange.

Stanley couldn't see the mountains from where he was, but he liked to imagine them there, and the Shenandoah Valley beyond. He hummed a few bars of an old song that his mother had sung, something about blue ridge mountains and lonesome pines.

Ever since he was a kid, pine trees had made Stanley feel lonesome. Maybe it was because of that song. That wasn't why he was feeling lonesome now, however, and the pines down by his creek weren't lonesome, either. There were plenty of other trees to keep them company: hickory, maple, and cedar, with dogwood scattered through them all. Stanley also had some apple and pear trees closer to the house. He was thinking about making his own cider and giving a complimentary bottle to his guests when they left.

He wished he could remember the rest of the song about the lonesome pine, but he couldn't come up with any more lines. They'd probably pop into his head in a day or so when he was least thinking about them. Things like that seemed to be happening to him a lot lately, something to do with getting older, he guessed.

He stood up. Time to go inside and check out the inn before he started feeling sorry for himself. When his first lodgers arrived, he wanted to be sure that everything was ready for them.

And it might be a good idea to see if there had been any cancellations. You could never tell about the power of television.

---

You can be sure that it will rain
when cats wash behind their ears.

When the cat sits with her tail
to the fire, bad weather
is on the way.

---

# 6

# Cats and Corn Bread

As soon as Stanley entered the front door, his cats came running to greet him. They had been Jane's cats originally, but he'd inherited them, and they seemed satisfied with the arrangement, as far as you could tell about cats. Stanley wasn't too sure about feline loyalty, but he had a feeling it wasn't strong.

Still, he liked the cats, and he had been careful to state in the inn's brochure that the cats lived there. He wasn't going to get rid of them, and he didn't want anyone with allergies to get a rude surprise.

Because of the grand opening festivities Stanley had kept the cats inside all day, both for their own safety and the safety of all the visitors to the inn's grounds. He wasn't sure how the cats would react to a crowd, and he was pretty sure they wouldn't like bluegrass music. He wouldn't want to be responsible if they became aggressive, since they were fully equipped with sharp teeth and claws, though missing certain other essential portions of their anatomies.

Binky and Cosmo were neutered toms, but that was where the resemblance between them ended. Binky was a huge gray tabby, tipping the scales at nearly twenty pounds. At Binky's last checkup, the vet had recommended that Binky be fed separately from the other cats and that he be given a special low-calorie, low-fat food.

Stanley had been slightly offended on Binky's behalf, but Binky minded not at all. He didn't seem to mind his new diet, either. As long as food of some kind was in his bowl, he wasn't particular about what kind it was.

Cosmo was the oldest of the three cats, almost sixteen. Cosmo weighed twelve pounds less than Binky, and when Stanley ran his hand down the old cat's backbone, he could feel its well-defined bumps just millimeters under the skin. Cosmo's color was a faded orange, and his once distinctive markings were now almost indistinguishable from the rest of his coat, which was a problem in itself. Cosmo seemed to shed his fur year-round and to walk in a cloud of lackluster orange hair that eventually wound up on the rugs, the furniture, and even the light fixtures. So far, Bill had managed to keep it picked up pretty well and hadn't complained about it. He liked cats, too.

Sheba was a spayed female. She was black-and-white and looked a little like the famous White House cat, Socks. Not that she cared. She walked through the world as if she were the only cat in it, and she demonstrated a supreme contempt for Binky and Cosmo, which was just fine with them, especially Cosmo, who as far as Stanley knew had never acknowledged her existence.

Stanley stooped down and rubbed them on their heads. Binky purred, Cosmo purred, and Sheba looked disdainful.

"Hungry, guys?" Stanley asked as he straightened up. "Come on."

They followed him down a short hall and turned right to go through the inn's parlor, which Stanley had furnished in 1930s style. The room held an old couch and some rockers, and across from the couch was an enormous fireplace that Stanley planned to use on cold winter nights.

As much as Stanley liked the fireplace, he was prouder of the big cabinet-model Philco radio. It looked as good as new, and it sounded even better. Of course it received only AM signals, but Stanley was convinced that the vacuum tubes inside it gave it the ability to pick up distant stations that a transistor radio couldn't begin to receive without an antenna. It wasn't easy to get tubes these days, but they could be found if you knew the right people, which Stanley did.

Another radio was in the parlor, too, one that looked a lot like the Philco, but it was a modern reproduction. It played AM, FM, cassette tapes, and CDs. Stanley didn't much like it, but he thought some of the guests might prefer it to the older model.

If they didn't, he also had an RCA Victrola, the kind you had to wind up, and some thick black phonograph records that were too scratchy to be of much use as entertainment.

There was no TV set. Stanley didn't feel that one would fit the decor. In fact, there wasn't a TV set in any of the guest rooms, either. He didn't know how the guests would react to that, but he supposed he'd find out.

The cats charged ahead of Stanley and into the dining room. The table was set for dinner, covered with a white cloth and the plain white china that Caroline Caldwell had picked out.

"Nobody uses the fancy china at home except on special occasions," she'd told Stanley. "And you want them to feel at home."

True, he thought, but after today's skinny-dipping event, he hoped that no one showed up at the table in boxer shorts and T-shirt.

He followed the cats into the kitchen, where Caroline Caldwell was cooking dinner. Bill was sitting at the small breakfast table, reading a copy of *Ellery Queen's Mystery Magazine.* A pot bubbled on the stove, and Stanley could smell the corn bread cooking in the oven.

"Beans?" he asked, looking at the pot.

"Pintos," Caroline said. She was a small, neat woman who wore her graying hair twisted into a knot on the back of her head. Stanley had never seen her without an apron. "We'll have a little bit of ham to go along with them. And corn bread."

"I can smell the corn bread," Stanley said. Thinking about it made his mouth water.

"What about Belinda?" Bill asked, closing his magazine and marking his place with his finger. "Did she get all right?"

Stanley looked over at the cats, all of whom were sitting in the door that led to the small utility room and watching him expectantly. He'd been putting off telling his staff about Belinda, but there was no getting around it now.

"No. She didn't get all right."

"Didn't think she would," Bill said.

Caroline opened the oven to check on the corn bread. "That woman," she said, shaking her head. "I always thought she'd try to get back at me some way, but not by dying in a bowl of my salsa."

"I don't think she did it deliberately," Stanley pointed out.

Caroline closed the oven. "Maybe not, but it'd be just like her. She was always a spiteful woman. Been that way ever since high school."

One thing Stanley had learned about living in a small town was that everyone there had a history. Feuds and friendships went back for years, sometimes for generations. It wasn't like the city, where you moved in and started from scratch. No one knew who you were, who your parents had been, or where you'd come from, and no one much cared.

Even Stanley had a history in Higgins. The first part of it ended with his high school graduation, and it picked up again with his return. The years between didn't seem to matter much to anyone.

"They still saying it might be a murder?" Bill asked.

"I didn't ask. They really wouldn't have any way of knowing so soon. But I don't think so. Who'd want to murder Belinda, anyway?"

To Stanley's surprise, Bill said, "Plenty of folks. You want a list?"

Caroline sniffed. "Don't speak ill of the dead," she told her husband. "There's no need of that."

"I guess not." Bill opened his magazine. "I'll tell you one thing, though. I'd a whole lot rather read about a murder than have one done while I'm standing around watching. It's not nearly so messy."

"We don't know that anyone has been murdered," Stanley said. "And that reminds me. Did we get any cancellations today?"

"Not a one," Caroline said. "So you'd better be ready in the morning for five couples to check in."

"I'm looking forward to it," Stanley said, though he wasn't looking forward to it as much as he had been earlier. "How long until we eat?"

"About ten minutes. You have time to feed those cats."

Caroline wasn't exactly fond of the cats. She'd told Stanley that she didn't want them underfoot in the kitchen. Stanley didn't want them there, either. He was afraid Cosmo would shed in the food. They had to walk through the room to get to the utility room where Stanley fed them, but that was as far as their kitchen privileges extended.

Stanley went into the utility room and got the

sack of dry food out of a cabinet. There was regular food for Cosmo and Sheba, while Binky got a special blend for "mature" cats in his bowl, which was set several feet away from the bowls used by the other two.

"What about the funeral?" Bill called from the kitchen as Stanley poured out the food.

"I haven't heard anything." The three cats started crunching their dinners. "I suppose John Jamar will handle the arrangements."

Jamar ran Jamar's Funeral Home, and he did the funerals for nearly everyone who died in Higgins.

"Are you planning to send flowers?" Caroline asked.

"I'll order them tomorrow."

"For the inn or just yourself?" Bill asked.

"For the inn, I guess."

"Be sure to put our names on the card," Bill said.

# 7

# Rooms with a View

The two-story building that housed Blue Skies was just on the outskirts of Higgins. When Stanley was growing up, the house had been just outside of the town limits, and he'd often seen it when he and his family were on one of their Sunday drives. He had liked the house even then, and he was pleased to be its owner now.

The house had been built sometime in the early part of the twentieth century. No one was sure exactly when, but the best guess was around 1910. The old-style farmhouse had a veranda on three sides. It was exactly what Stanley had been looking for when he decided to become an innkeeper. It was picturesque and appealing now, completely rebuilt and freshly painted, though it had taken a good bit of imagination to see its appealing qualities before all the restoration work had begun.

Stanley's room was on the ground floor, and all five guest rooms were on the second floor. Two bathrooms were up there, so of course the guests had to share. That was to be expected in a bed-and-breakfast, however, and none of those making reservations had complained so far. Stanley had his own bathroom, but he felt that was his privilege as the owner. Besides, he had to share his whole room with the cats.

Usually the cats slept fairly quietly in their separate baskets lined up against the wall near Stanley's dresser, but Hal Tipton had built a special cat entrance into the back door so the cats could go out if they felt the urge. Sometimes they got restless and used it, though they seldom disturbed Stanley when they did so. They seemed to prefer to go out in the daytime and lie in the sun or creep around to eye the birds, their tails switching back and forth. Stanley had blocked the entrance earlier in the day, but after eating more ham, beans, and corn bread than was probably good for him, he made sure that it was open. He didn't want the cats waking him in the middle of the night.

Then, while Bill cleared up in the kitchen, Stanley went upstairs to have one last look at the guest rooms. Each one had been named for a president born in Virginia: the Washington Room, the Jefferson Room, the Madison Room, the Monroe Room, and the Wilson Room.

Stanley felt a little guilty about slighting the other three Virginia-born presidents—Tyler, Harrison, and Taylor—but he thought it would be best to go with the five that most people would know a little about.

Each room had a portrait of the appropriate president on the wall, but that was the only reference to the name of the room to be found. Mostly the names existed only in Stanley's head.

All the rooms were filled with old furniture that Stanley had found in antique stores around Higgins, though none of the furniture was actually from the plantation period. The beds were spread with colorful handmade quilts (Stanley had been appalled at the prices), and a quilt stand was beside each bed. On the dressers there were washbasins and pitchers, though Stanley didn't know whether anyone would actually use them. There was even a chamber pot under the bed in the Washington Room. Like the washbasins, it was there strictly for looks, or so Stanley fervently hoped.

Besides the portraits, each room had its distinguishing feature. The Jefferson Room had a canopy bed, while a Franklin stove was in the Monroe

Room. Stanley was sure Monroe wouldn't have minded. The Madison Room had a parquet floor that Hal Tipton had laid. And the Wilson Room had a marble-topped dresser and nightstand. It was the only room without a fireplace, however.

Stanley looked into every room. They were all immaculate, and he was sure that his first guests were going to be pleased with their accommodations. He hoped none of them had watched *Hello, World!* earlier that day.

Or maybe it wouldn't matter if they had. Stanley had no way of knowing just how much of the Belinda incident had made it onto the air. He figured that the producer wouldn't have aired more than a total of fifteen minutes about the inn, not counting Stanley's guest shot as weatherman for the day. Possibly the footage of Belinda hadn't been broadcast at all, even as sensational as it was. Maybe they'd been away for a commercial when she took her dive.

Of course there was always tomorrow. As soon as the network got the news that Belinda was dead, the footage of her toppling into the salsa would be run and rerun every hour, and not just on the network. The news channels would love it.

Stanley had once heard that there was no such thing as bad publicity, and there was a time that he'd even believed it. Now he wasn't at all sure that was true.

Satisfied with the rooms, he went back downstairs to say good-night to Bill and Caroline. They had finished in the kitchen and were just about to go out to their own rooms, located in a separate building next to the barn. The realtor had referred to the apartment as the "servants' quarters," but Stanley didn't feel that the term was appropriate. He thought of Bill and Caroline as his friends, so he simply called the place their "apartment." That seemed to suit them fine.

Hal Tipton had his own house in town, and he preferred to live there, though Stanley had offered to build him an apartment in the barn. Hal drove out to the inn every day to do his work and drove back when he was done.

"Big day tomorrow," Bill said. "I know you're looking forward to it."

"It was a lot of work getting this place ready," Caroline added. "And you've put a lot of money into it, too."

"It's not the money," Stanley said honestly.

For reasons that he wasn't sure about, he was known as a tight man with a dollar, but he wasn't becoming an innkeeper to make money. He had plenty of money, and the inn was just a way to keep busy and surround himself with what he hoped would be a lot of different groups of interesting people whom he could entertain, feed, and make happy for a few days.

"Well, money or not, I hope everything goes well," Bill said. "And I hope we don't have any more excitement like that business today."

"Me, too," Stanley said. "I've had enough excitement to last me for a while."

"What about that stage Hal built out there?" Caroline asked. "Are you going to leave it?"

"I'll have to think about it. We might want to use it again. We could have square-dancing lessons for the guests, or maybe have the cloggers out some evening."

Bill said, "I'd think most of your guests would want to be traveling around, seeing things like Mount Vernon, not taking dancing lessons or watching those cloggers."

"Well, we'll have to learn as we go along," Stanley said. "Anyway, I'd like to have some community events out here, get people in town used to coming around. I want us to have a good relationship with everyone in Higgins."

"We didn't make a very good start today," Caroline said, "what with Belinda and all."

"I wouldn't say that," Bill told her. "There might be some that say we did the town a favor."

"We didn't do anything," Caroline said. "And don't you start saying bad things about the dead again. You know that's not right. Even if it is Belinda you're talking about."

"I'll try to do better," Bill said. "Anyway, another way to look at it is that things can't get much worse."

"Thanks for cheering me up," Stanley said.

Bill smiled. "Anytime." He picked up his magazine from the table. "Guess we'll be going on to bed now. See you in the morning."

"I'm looking forward to it," Stanley said.

And in spite of all that had happened, he was. He'd been getting ready for more than a year, and no matter what had happened to Belinda, there was always tomorrow, which, as Scarlett O'Hara had said, was another day.

Stanley wondered what the weather would be like, then laughed at himself. It would be beautiful; he was sure of that. And wasn't he a weatherman?

# 8

# Early to Rise

The next day Stanley got up at 4:30 A.M. He'd gotten up every day at that time when he was a kid living on a farm just outside of Higgins, and he'd never lost the habit. Unlike some of his habits, that one had stood him in good stead. He'd never had trouble getting up for the early-morning radio shows he'd done at the beginning of his career, and he'd easily adapted to the *Hello, World!* schedule that some of the other cast members found almost impossible.

Since these days there was really nothing to do at such an early hour, Stanley usually sat in his rocker and read for a while. He read a little of everything, from best-sellers to the Bible, depending on his mood. Today, after the events of the day before, he felt that the Bible would be a good choice, and he read a great deal of the book of Proverbs. Chapter 30, verse 18 caught his eye particularly:

*There are three things which are too wonderful for me,*
*Four which I do not understand:*
*The way of an eagle in the sky,*
*The way of a serpent on a rock,*
*The way of a ship in the middle of the sea,*
*And the way of a man with a maid.*

For some reason the last line made him think of Marilyn Tunney again. He wondered if she liked to get up early. Probably not. Most people didn't, not even Jane, though she'd always tried to be awake when Stanley left the house. He remembered the way she would smile at him from the bed, and once he'd jumped right back under the covers with her. It was the only time in his career he'd been late for work, and he'd never regretted it.

When the sky began to lighten, Stanley put the Bible aside, took a shower, and got dressed. Then he looked out the bedroom window.

The day was even more beautiful than the previous one, if that was possible. Without the aid of the National Weather Service, Stanley predicted that it would be mostly sunny, with a high temperature in the middle seventies. It was a safe enough prediction, and if it was wrong, no one would care since no one had heard it.

Stanley went to the kitchen and celebrated his opening day by letting Caroline fix him a ranch omelette, a treat that he didn't often allow himself. He even put a little extra butter and salt in the grits that accompanied the omelette. And he buttered his toast, too.

After he'd eaten, he complimented Caroline on her culinary skills and put out some food for the cats. He asked Caroline not to let Binky get into the wrong bowl and went out for his daily walk around the grounds. He walked down to the creek, enjoying the cool depths of the early-morning shadows and the smell of the pines. He wished that it were a little earlier in the year and the dogwood were blooming.

He picked up a stick, tossed it in the creek, and watched it float slowly away. The creek was small, not more than a couple of yards wide, but it had clear, moving water in it all year. It was shallow, though there were pools several feet deep in places, and the pools sometimes held fish. It was fed by a little spring that was also on Stanley's property, and that had led to another of his small projects, or rather one of Hal's projects, the building of a springhouse.

Of course the springhouse wouldn't be used in place of modern refrigeration, but it was something that Stanley wanted to have on the place to show his guests, most of whom, he was sure, would never have seen anything quite like it. Stanley had seen one often when he was young, on his grandmother's farm. It had kept milk and butter just as nice as a modern refrigerator.

Another of Stanley's projects was the smokehouse. It was out by the barn, and Stanley definitely planned to use it to smoke his own hams. There was nothing better than a home-smoked ham, if the curing was done right, and Stanley had inherited the secret of doing it right from his grandfather. All he needed now was a ham, but that would come in the fall.

He walked back up past the barn, which was used only for storage, since Stanley wasn't interested in raising any livestock other than his three cats. Behind the barn, at one end, was the compost pile. Stanley believed in doing things the old-fashioned way when he could, and so far he had used no chemical fertilizers or pesticides on his garden.

Taking the pitchfork leaning against the barn

wall, Stanley gave the compost pile a few turns, inhaling its rich odor as he did so. It wasn't as pleasant as the smell of the pines, but it had its charms if you were in the right frame of mind, and Stanley was usually in the right frame of mind early in the morning.

He replaced the pitchfork and walked on around the barn and past the smokehouse to the garden. The corn wasn't quite as high as an elephant's eye, but it would soon be up to Stanley's shoulder. The cucumbers and snap beans were coming along, and the few tomatoes that were left were turning from green to red. They would have to be picked soon, and Stanley wondered what he would do with them. He wouldn't have Caroline make any salsa, that was for sure.

Near the garden was the little goldfish pond that Hal Tipton had put in. The clear water had a few lily pads floating on it, but Stanley could see the bright orange fish swimming just below the surface. He wondered how long it would be before one of the cats tried to catch one.

Probably quite a while, since the cats seemed content with what Stanley fed them. As far as he knew, they hadn't made any attempts to supplement their diets with fish any more than with birds, not even Binky. All three of them were sleeping in the sun on the small back porch when Stanley got back to the house. Sheba was lying practically on top of Binky, and his front leg was thrown across her body. They hardly moved when Stanley passed by them and into the house.

Bill was eating a breakfast of scrambled eggs and bacon when Stanley entered the kitchen. The bacon smelled so good that Stanley wished he'd had some himself. A copy of the morning paper from Alexandria was lying on the table.

"There's good news and bad news," Bill said.

Stanley stopped by the table, but he didn't look down at the paper. "Give me the good news."

Bill tapped the paper with a finger. "Belinda didn't make the front page."

Stanley smiled. "All right. Now give me the bad news."

"Blue Skies didn't make the front page, either."

Stanley was disappointed and his face showed it. "It didn't?"

"Nope, but it did make the front page of the lifestyle section."

Bill picked up the first section of the paper so Stanley could see the one that lay beneath it. There was a picture of the inn, with the caption "Blue Skies Ahead."

"Did you read the article?"

"Yep. It's real nice, says a lot of good things about you and about Blue Skies. It even mentions Little Melvin and the band."

That was good. Little Melvin would be pleased.

"What about Belinda?"

"Well, that's part of the bad news. There's a sidebar about her dying, and she's in the obituaries, of course."

Stanley stuck out his hand for the paper. "I guess I'd better read about it."

Bill handed Stanley the paper, and he looked at the sidebar first. It wasn't so bad, except for the sentence that said, "Police have not ruled out the possibility of foul play."

"Could've been worse," Bill said, watching Stanley's face.

Stanley put the paper down on the table. "I guess so. I just wish it hadn't happened at all. Poor Belinda."

Bill snorted. "I keep telling you that nobody's going to miss Belinda. You were gone for a while, and you haven't had any dealings with her since you got back, so you don't know about her. But she wasn't anybody's favorite person."

"I seem to remember that she got engaged a lot," Stanley said. "Somebody must've liked her."

"Sure she got engaged, but she never got married. Do you remember that, too?"

Stanley said that he did. "I never really knew why, though."

Bill opened his mouth to tell him, but just then Caroline came into the room.

"Are you finished with those eggs yet?" she asked.

"Just about." Bill shoveled in the last couple of bites and picked up the last piece of bacon. "I was just about to tell Stanley why Belinda never got married."

Caroline pursed her lips. "I don't hold with gossiping. You clean up this kitchen now and let Mr. Waters get on with his business."

Bill snapped the bacon in two and popped half of it in his mouth. He chewed it slowly and winked at Stanley as if to say, "I'll tell you later."

Stanley hoped he would. He didn't hold with gossip, either, but he was curious about Belinda. It wouldn't be gossiping, exactly. It would be exchanging information.

"Is Hal coming out today?" Caroline asked.

"Not unless we need him," Stanley told her. "He says everything's working just fine."

"I hope so," she said. "I wouldn't want anything to spoil today."

"I don't think you have to worry about that," Stanley said. "What could go wrong?"

He was on his way to the front porch when the telephone rang.

# 9

# Poison

The phone was on a small rolltop desk in Stanley's bedroom, which was large enough to double as the inn's office. He stopped, turned back, and went into his room to answer it. He was pleasantly surprised when he learned that his caller was Marilyn Tunney.

"How are you, Stanley?"

"Great. Couldn't be better. I'm really looking forward to the rest of the day. The first guests should be checking in around ten o'clock."

"That's nice."

Marilyn didn't sound particularly interested, and Stanley's pleasant feeling faded away. "I'll bet you didn't call just to find out when my guests were arriving."

"Well, not exactly. I do care about that, though."

Stanley felt the top of his head turning red. "Really?"

"Of course. We're old friends. That's why I hate to get to the official part of this call."

"What's the official part?"

"The part about Belinda."

"You've already told me about Belinda. And it was in the paper today. I was really sorry to hear it."

"That's not all, Stanley."

Stanley didn't feel his head getting red anymore. Instead he felt his breakfast omelette turning to concrete in his stomach.

"Tell me the rest."

"Belinda was poisoned."

Stanley had been standing by the desk. Now he sat in the desk chair, took a deep breath, let out a little air, and said, "Are you sure?"

"The autopsy was done last night. I just got the report. There's no doubt about it."

"How?"

"Boric acid. But I'm not going to tell that to everyone."

"Boric acid?"

"A lot of it. It must have been in something she ate. The coroner says that there was quite a bit in her system. She couldn't have lived for long after ingesting it."

"Could she have committed suicide?"

"That doesn't seem very likely. The amount she ingested would have acted very quickly, and I don't think she would have chosen Blue Skies as a place to kill herself. I've called the lab and asked them to rush their analysis of the food."

Stanley ran a hand across the top of his head. "I don't understand. Why on earth would anyone want to poison Belinda?"

"That's what I'll have to find out. She must have been the target, since no one else was affected. Do you know what else that means?"

Stanley thought about it, but he couldn't come up with anything.

So Marilyn told him. "It means that whoever put the poison in the food must have been nearby."

"How could they put poison in the food?"

"It wouldn't have been hard. Boric acid in powder form is used for killing insects. Like cockroaches. It dissolves in water, and someone could have poured it in the food. I'd bet on the salsa. Something spicy like that would conceal the taste very easily, and there wasn't really anything else on the table that would have worked."

Stanley couldn't think of anything to say, and there was a brief pause.

Then Marilyn said, "Where were you standing, Stanley?"

"Well, let me see. . . . Bill Caldwell and I—wait a minute."

Stanley stopped and thought about what Hal Tipton had said about Marilyn not trusting anyone.

"You don't suspect me, do you? I hardly knew Belinda!"

"Of course I don't suspect you," Marilyn said, but Stanley didn't believe her. He'd seen plenty of cop shows on television, and he knew that the cops always suspected everyone. Hal Tipton was right. On the other hand, she'd told him about the boric acid.

"I just thought that you might have seen something," Marilyn said. "Maybe you noticed who was standing by the table, someone who might have had an opportunity to put the poison in the salsa bowl."

Stanley's feelings were hurt, but he tried not to let that show in his voice.

"I was talking to Bill. I didn't see anyone, and I don't see how it's possible for anyone to have done it."

"The poison could have been in a bottle, any kind of bottle. Did you see anyone carrying a bottle of designer drinking water, for example?"

Stanley couldn't remember, but then he wasn't a trained observer like the police were supposed to be. And he hadn't been expecting anyone to be murdered right there at one of his tables.

"The thing of it is," he said, "there must have been forty or fifty people around Belinda. There were that many when I got to her, all trying to see what the trouble was."

"And trying not to look guilty."

"I really don't like talking about this."

"I don't blame you. But you're going to have to talk about it. Someone at your party is a killer."

Stanley leaned back in the chair and sighed. It had been bad enough to have Belinda die. Now it was murder, and someone he had invited to his celebration was a killer. That really bothered him. And the media were going to love this. He was going to get more free publicity than he'd ever hoped for.

And all of it was going to be bad.

"Couldn't she have gotten it somewhere else?" he asked.

"It was poison, Stanley. Can you say *poison*?"

He didn't want to say it, but he did. "Couldn't she have been poisoned somewhere else?"

"Not according to the coroner. The amount she had would have finished her off too quickly. She might possibly have eaten it at some other table, but there wasn't another table."

"Could she have drunk it?"

"In what? She didn't have anything with her. What kind of drinks did you have?"

"Lemonade. I think your Officer Kunkel carried some away for analysis. But it must be all right. Lots of people drank it."

"So it wasn't in the lemonade. Face it, Stanley. It was in the salsa."

"Damn."

"I sort of feel the same way. We don't have a lot of murders in Higgins."

"Well, excuse me."

Marilyn laughed. "I'm not blaming you, Stanley. Whoever killed Belinda would have done it somewhere else if not at Blue Skies."

"I wish he had."

"He? Who said anything about 'he'?"

"Excuse me again."

"Don't be so humble, Stanley. It doesn't become you."

It was Stanley's turn to laugh. "I guess it

doesn't, at that. All right. I'm sorry. It's just that you sort of ruined my big day."

"Well, excuse me."

This time they both laughed, and for reasons he didn't feel like analyzing, Stanley felt the top of his head getting red again.

"Listen, Stanley," Marilyn said, her tone becoming serious, "I'm hoping you'll give me some help on this."

"Help? Me? I don't know anything about solving murders. I'm not Jessica Fletcher."

"I don't expect you to be. I was thinking more along the lines of getting you to try a little harder to remember who was near that table. And you might ask Bill Caldwell, too."

"Bill?"

"He was with you, wasn't he?"

"Oh. Right."

"Well, he might remember seeing something that you don't recall. I could talk to him myself, but sometimes people are a little uneasy around the police."

"I can't imagine why."

"Oh, yes, you can. It's what we call our 'command presence.' Will you talk to him?"

"Sure. And I'll try to jog my own miserable memory."

"Thanks, Stanley. I really appreciate it. I'll come out later and talk to you in person."

"I'll look forward to it." Stanley meant it, even if the occasion for her visit was going to be the investigation of a murder case.

# 10

# Arrivals

Stanley told Bill and Caroline the bad news, but they didn't have time to discuss it for long because Stanley's guests began to arrive.

Mr. and Mrs. Larry Ferguson from Texas were the first to check in, and Mrs. Ferguson ("You call me Sandy, now, you hear?") was more impressed by the quilt in the Washington Room than she was by meeting Stanley.

"Look at that, Larry!" she said, pointing with red-tipped nails. "That's the wedding-ring pattern. My grandmother had a quilt just like that on her bed when I was a little girl. Hers didn't use the same colors, but the pattern was exactly the same. Isn't that wonderful?"

Larry agreed that it was wonderful.

"And that's just the cutest little washbasin. You see that, Larry? Can we use it, Mr. Waters?"

Stanley asked her to call him Stanley and explained about the shared bathrooms. He said that they could use the basin if they wanted to.

"You go right down to that bathroom and fill it, Larry," Sandy told her husband, who took the basin and left without a word.

"Lunch in an hour and a half," Stanley said. "Real home cooking."

"I'll bet it's just as good as that brochure of yours made it look, too. I can hardly wait."

"I'm sure you won't be disappointed," Stanley said, and left to allow her to get unpacked.

Before noon, the Campbells from Iowa ("You look just like on TV!"), the Stuttses from California ("We'd recognize that voice anywhere!"), the Jacksons from New York ("Isn't this the neatest little place?"), and the Brodnaxes from Louisiana ("Would you mind standing over there with Toni while I take a picture?") had all arrived and gotten settled.

At lunch everyone all gathered around the big dining table, with Stanley at the head, and tucked into a meal of roast beef cooked with potatoes and carrots, homemade whole-wheat rolls with country butter, and chocolate pie for dessert.

It wasn't exactly the kind of meal that a health-conscious eater like Stanley wanted to serve as a regular thing, but he'd thought it would be a good idea to kick things off with something comfortable and homey. No one had any objections, especially not after they'd tasted Caroline's pie, which reduced Mr. Brodnax to a state of eye-rolling ecstasy.

After lunch, all the guests returned to their rooms, where Stanley imagined that at least half of them would take naps induced by the midday meal, while the other half organized the rest of the day.

For everyone, the rest of the day would most likely consist of sight-seeing expeditions. The inn was within a short distance of two interstate highways that led to any number of historical sites, including Mount Vernon and several Civil War battlefields, such as Manassas, Fredericksburg, Chancellorsville, and Spotsylvania Court House.

Or the sight-seeing could be combined with shopping in Higgins itself, which had numerous antique stores and a rich heritage. Its town square had two statues on it: one a memorial to the dead of the Revolutionary War and the other to the dead of the Civil War.

Stanley hoped everyone was gone by the time Marilyn Tunney arrived. He didn't want his guests to see him being questioned by the police.

When everyone was safely upstairs, Stanley

went into the kitchen, where Bill Caldwell was loading the lunch dishes into the dishwasher and Caroline was seated at the table, already beginning her preparations for supper, which is what Stanley had decided the meal would be called at his inn. Supper was the meal you ate at home with your family; dinner was what you ate when you dressed up and went out.

He had planned from the beginning to serve three meals a day at his inn if the guests wanted them. Great food was one of his major selling points.

"That was a wonderful meal, Caroline," Stanley said. "I think that pie may be the best you ever made, and that's saying a lot. If Mr. Brodnax hadn't had his wife with him, he might have come right in here and proposed marriage to you."

"Wouldn't have done him any good," Bill said. "She's taken."

Caroline looked up from the menu she was working on.

"You wouldn't deny a woman the chance to improve herself, would you?" she asked her husband.

"I would if it meant I wasn't going to get any more of that pie." Bill clinked the last plate in the dishwasher and closed the door.

"Did you remember to put in the soap?" Caroline looked at Stanley and nodded toward her husband. "Last night he forgot the soap. Had to wash everything over this morning."

"That business with Belinda shook me up some," Bill said.

"You never did tell me why she'd been engaged so often but never married," Stanley reminded him.

"And he's not going to tell you now," Caroline said.

Bill sat at the table across from his wife. "I don't know why you're taking up for Belinda. You and she never did get along even when you were kids."

Stanley remembered something Bill had said the previous day. "Were the two of you in the same home ec class?"

Caroline nodded. "That's right. Belinda never could cook, but she always wanted to be the best. She might have been a little jealous of me. It didn't amount to anything."

"Never could beat you at the fair, either," Bill added. "That's not all, though."

"You might as well tell me," Stanley said. "You've danced around it for so long that you've got me imagining all sorts of things."

"Bill's just overly proud of himself," Caroline said. "He thinks the reason Belinda's never married is that she never got over him. Going with him ruined other men for her."

Stanley gave Bill a grin. "Ah. So you dated Belinda yourself?"

"You wouldn't remember, I guess, you being a little younger than we are. But Belinda and I were quite an item for a while there. Before I started dating Caroline, that is. After that, I was a one-woman man."

"Belinda didn't see it that way," Caroline said. "She couldn't stand to be second best in anything, whether it was catching men or making jelly."

"That was a long time ago, though," Stanley said, thinking it must have been at least twenty years since he'd heard anyone refer to "catching a man." "Surely Belinda got over it."

"You didn't know Belinda very well, did you?" Bill said. "I'll tell you the truth—"

Caroline held up a warning hand. "You won't tell anybody anything, Bill Caldwell. That poor woman's dead, and we're going to let her rest in peace."

"I guess you're right," Bill said. "Folks could get the wrong idea if we said too much."

Stanley had been mildly curious up to this

point, but now he was getting really interested. He wanted to ask a few more questions, but before he got the chance, someone knocked at the front door.

If trees keep their leaves until late in the fall,
a bad winter will follow.

A mild November means a bad winter.

If the fruit trees bloom in fall,
the winter will be cold.

# 11

# Come into My Parlor

Stanley went to the door and opened it for Marilyn Tunney. Stanley was glad that none of the guests was around, though it didn't really matter. Marilyn wasn't in uniform.

Stanley thought she looked wonderful. Her eyes were still as blue as any he'd ever seen, and her skin was as smooth as it had ever been. She was considerably shorter than Stanley, about nine inches less than his six feet and an inch or so, and she didn't look as if she needed to worry much about her diet.

"May I come in, or are we going to stand out here and look at each other?"

The top of Stanley's head got red and he backed out of the doorway. "I'm sorry. I didn't know you were looking at me."

Marilyn followed him into the hall. "You look pretty good, Stanley, you know that?"

"For a man my age, you mean?"

"I didn't say that."

"It just seems I've gotten to that age. You know, the age where people say, 'You're looking good,' when what they really mean is, 'I'm surprised to see you still walking around.' "

"You've got a long way to go before you get to that age, Stanley. You really do look good."

Stanley ran a hand over his head. It felt as if he'd been in the sun for an hour or two without a cap on. He hoped the redness wouldn't seep down to his face.

"Well, I've been trying to eat right, and I go for a walk every day."

They went into the parlor, and Marilyn said, "That's not what I meant. I meant it was good to see you, and it's nice to know that you're going to be living in Higgins again."

Stanley, who had made his living by talking for more years than he cared to remember, couldn't think of a thing to say. He had always prided himself on his ability to ad-lib, but for the first time in his life he found himself wishing someone were standing across from him with a handful of cue cards.

"This is a lovely room," Marilyn said, looking around and taking it in. "Are those radios real antiques?"

Stanley explained that one of them was. "The other one plays tapes and CDs, but I have mostly music from the 1950s. I have some tapes of old radio shows, too, if anyone wants to hear them."

"I wouldn't mind hearing them myself, sometime."

Stanley tried not to stammer. "You'd be welcome anytime. How about now?"

"Well, I didn't really come here for a social visit."

Stanley was a little disappointed, but he said, "I knew that. Why don't we sit down."

They sat on the couch, Stanley at one end, Marilyn at the other.

"I haven't really thought of anything that would help you," Stanley said. The top of his head was back to its normal temperature. "I can remember some of the people I saw in the crowd, but they weren't especially near the table."

"Anything you can tell me would help." Marilyn opened her purse and took out a small spiral notebook and a pen. "So far I don't have the name of a single person who was nearby."

"I don't want to implicate anyone. It wouldn't

be right. I just don't have any way of knowing who was there when Belinda was . . . poisoned and who had just walked over out of curiosity when she fell."

"I'm not going to hound anyone, Stanley. I just need a little help, a starting place. That's all. I'm not going to put anyone in jail just for being in the wrong place at the wrong time. Some of the people you saw might have valuable information that I won't be able to get unless I talk to them. And I can't talk to them if I don't know their names."

Stanley thought it over. It made sense when you thought about it the way Marilyn explained it.

"All right. Hal Tipton was there, for one."

Marilyn wrote something in her notebook. "Hal works for you, doesn't he?"

"Not full-time. But he's done a lot of work here at the inn, and he's sort of on call."

Marilyn wrote some more in the notebook, then looked up. "All right. Who else?"

"Jim Nugent was giving Belinda CPR when I got to her."

As Marilyn began to write, Stanley watched her closely, but as far as he could tell, Nugent's name didn't cause any special reaction. Maybe he hadn't called her about that date yet.

Marilyn looked up. "Next?"

"Well, I remember Corey Gainer saying something to me."

Marilyn wrote, then looked at Stanley encouragingly. "What did he say?"

"Something about Belinda gobbling the salsa. I wasn't paying much attention."

Marilyn wrote. When she finished she said, "Okay. I've got it. Go on."

"Barry Miller was there with Tommy Bright. No surprise there. Where you see one, you see the other. They're like Tweedledum and Tweedledee."

He wondered if she'd write that last comment down. Probably not. It wasn't very policelike.

"Anybody else?"

"Lacy Falk was talking to Ellen Winston. Ellen looked pretty upset."

"She would be. She and Belinda were friends. But maybe you knew that."

Stanley said that he did, and that he couldn't remember anyone else who'd been around Belinda.

"You're sure? Try hard."

"I'm sorry, but—wait a second. There was a TV cameraman there. I don't know his name, but I'm sure I could find out if you need it."

"I don't think he'd be much of a suspect, being from out of town," Marilyn said, but she wrote something in the notebook anyway.

"Do you want me to get in touch with the network?"

"Not yet." Marilyn folded her notebook and put it back in her purse. "There's another possibility, you know."

"There is?"

"Two, really. I'm sure you can figure it out."

Stanley tried, and after a second or two he saw what she was getting at. He didn't much like it. "You're talking about the person who made the salsa. And the person who put it on the table."

"Not bad. Two people, unless the same person did both things. You could be a pretty good detective if you wanted to."

"I don't think I want to, not when my friends are involved."

"I don't much blame you. I feel pretty much the same way, but it comes with the job."

"Surely you don't think Bill or Caroline had anything to do with Belinda's death."

"I have to check everything, no matter what I think. Are they both involved?"

"Caroline made the salsa. Bill carried everything out and put it on the table."

Stanley remembered that Bill had been in sort of a hurry to carry the bowl of salsa away, too. He didn't remind Marilyn, however. She'd been there, and she would have noticed. She was a trained observer.

"Could I talk to Bill and Caroline? Are they here?"

Stanley nodded. "They're probably in the kitchen."

"Did you know of any bad feeling between them and Belinda?"

Stanley said, "Nothing recent."

And then he wished he hadn't said anything at all, because Marilyn immediately asked him what he meant.

Stanley had a brief inner struggle. He always tried to tell the truth; that was one of his basic principles. But he didn't want to say anything that would make Marilyn suspicious of Bill and Caroline.

In the end the truth won out. "Bill dated Belinda before he met Caroline. According to them, Belinda's been jealous ever since. But I don't see how some high school romance could cause a murder so many years later."

Marilyn looked Stanley in the eyes. "Don't you think high school romances can be very compelling?"

Stanley's head began heating up again. "Well, ah, I guess some of them can."

Marilyn stood up. "Then I suppose I should talk to Caroline and Bill. But I want to talk to them separately. Could you go in the kitchen and ask one of them to come out here?"

Stanley could, but he didn't want to. On the other hand, he couldn't see any way out of it. Then he thought of something else.

"Wait a minute. How could they have known that Belinda would eat the salsa? The bowl was right there on the table. Anyone could have dipped a chip or two in it."

Marilyn gave him a round of silent applause. "I knew you had the makings of a good detective. Your only problem is that you don't think things all the way through. Do you want me to tell you?"

Stanley shook his head. "No. Give me a second."

It took him more than a second, but when the answer came to him, he thought it was the right one.

"In the first place, I don't believe for a minute that either Bill or Caroline had a thing to do with what happened. But if Caroline did, she couldn't have been in it alone. Bill would have to have known."

"That's right. And he could have waited until Belinda was standing right by the salsa to put it on the table. And then he could have said, 'Why don't you try this? It's delicious.' "

"And of course he could have done the same thing, only on his own. Caroline wouldn't have had to know."

"Right again."

"There's only one thing wrong with that idea. Bill was with me when Belinda collapsed."

"How long had he been with you?"

"What difference does— Oh. I see what you mean."

"We call it establishing an alibi. He puts the bowl down, tells Belinda to help herself, and then finds someone who'll say, 'Oh, no, Bill couldn't have done it. He was with me.'"

"Did anyone ever tell you that you have a really perverse view of human nature?"

"Now and then. But having a perverse view of human nature is just part of being a cop. We don't always see people on their best behavior. Unlike you. I'm sure that people in the television business are practically angels."

"Well, I wouldn't say that."

"I didn't think you would. But I'll admit that my view of life might be a little darker than yours. Sometimes, anyway."

"Do you like having an outlook like that?"

"No. But I've gotten used to it. Besides, when I'm not working, I can be a very optimistic person. You'll see."

Stanley rubbed his head. "I'll see?"

"Yes. But not right now. Right now I need to talk to Caroline and Bill. Would you mind asking one of them to come in here?"

Stanley stood up. "I'll go see if they're still in the kitchen."

He started out of the parlor, then stopped and turned back to Marilyn.

"There's one more person."

Marilyn nodded. "I know."

"You do?"

"We talked about it earlier. You."

"So what do you want to ask me?"

Marilyn smiled. She had a nice smile, with little crinkles at the corners of her eyes.

"Nothing. I trust you, Stanley."

Stanley started to rub his head, stopped himself, and then once again he couldn't think of a single witty remark. So he just said, "Thanks."

# 12

# Questions

Caroline was still sitting at the table, but Bill had already gone.

"He went out to the apartment to take a nap," Caroline said when Stanley asked. "He's probably dreaming about the old days with Belinda."

Stanley wondered if that was true. "Marilyn Tunney's here. She'd like to talk to you."

Caroline stood up. "I'm not surprised. I was wondering when she'd get around to it. After all, I was the one who made that salsa."

Stanley was a little taken aback at how calm she was. "Doesn't it bother you to be questioned by the police?"

"Not one single bit. Why should it? My conscience is clear."

"I never doubted it. Marilyn's in the parlor."

"I'll go talk to her, and you can go wake up Bill.

He won't thank you for it, but Marilyn will want to talk to him, too."

"I'll get him."

Stanley went out the back way as Caroline headed into the parlor. The cats were stretched out in the sun in the backyard. They were all sleeping peacefully, plainly not worrying about a thing, and completely oblivious to a jay that was shrilling somewhere down by the creek.

At times like this, Stanley wished he were a cat. Cats had it pretty easy. They got to eat when they were hungry and lie in the sun when they were sleepy. They didn't have to worry about things like murder.

On the other hand, he thought, being a cat wasn't all fun. He was pretty sure he wouldn't like being neutered, especially considering the way he'd been feeling about Marilyn. The top of his head got warm again.

He knocked on the door of the apartment, and when there was no answer, he knocked again. This time he thought he heard someone shuffling around, and he waited patiently until Bill came to the door, stuffing in his shirttail and trying to look as if he hadn't been asleep.

"What's the problem?" he asked, standing in the doorway.

"Marilyn Tunney wants to talk with you."

"Oh. Right now?"

"Not quite yet. She's talking to Caroline first."

"Oh. Well, do you want to come in, or should we wait in the inn?"

"We should probably wait over there. We can sit in the kitchen."

"All right." Bill came outside. "I guess I can see why she'd want to talk to us."

"It's just routine," Stanley said, thinking he sounded like someone on *Dragnet*.

As they strolled toward the inn, Bill said, "You know, I like to read mystery stories. Like the ones in that Ellery Queen magazine. Sometimes people in those stories get poisoned, but I don't really know anything about it."

"Do you remember the method the poisoner used in any of the stories?" Stanley told himself that he wasn't suspicious of Bill. Asking a question didn't mean anything.

"Nope. We have a few kinds of poison around here, you know."

Stanley hadn't known. "We do?"

"Sure. We use it for killing bugs, roaches mainly. Just put a little out where the cats can't get to it and it's perfectly safe."

They stopped to look at the cats, and Stanley

bent down to run a hand over Sheba, who of course didn't appreciate it as much as Binky or Cosmo would have. She didn't purr, but her black fur was warm from the sun.

"You're sure the cats can't get into it?"

"Yeah. It's Hal that puts it out, though, not me. We don't have much trouble with bugs in the house. I keep things too clean for that. We get some in the barn, though."

Stanley turned his attentions to Cosmo, and a fine haze of dull orange fur rose into the air as he stroked the old cat's side.

"You need to brush that cat," Bill said. "Get rid of some of that loose hair. It's a wonder he doesn't have hair balls the size of walnuts."

Stanley hadn't seen Cosmo hacking up anything, and he hadn't noticed any hair balls lying around. He'd have to ask the vet about that when he took Cosmo in for his shots. And maybe he'd give the cat a good brushing, too. But right now his mind was on something else.

"Where do we keep that poison?" he asked, rubbing Binky now.

"Out in the barn. It's boric acid, I think."

Stanley thought he did a masterful job of keeping his face blank. It made sense that the poison would be in the barn, since the barn was used primarily as a storage area. That way the boric acid would be well out of the way of the cats.

Stanley straightened and told himself that he would check on the boric acid supply when he got a chance.

Bill must have read his mind. "It's in a big round yellow-and-black cardboard can, up high on that shelf to the right when you first go inside. You can't miss it."

"There's no way it could have gotten into the salsa, is there?"

"Not unless somebody put it there. Caroline wouldn't let anything like that in her kitchen."

Stanley opened the back door and held it for Bill to go in. Stanley looked back at the cats, who showed no inclination to move inside, or to move at all for that matter. Bill went straight to the kitchen table and sat down.

"You know," he said when Stanley joined him, "I didn't tell you the whole story about Belinda."

Stanley said that he knew.

"Caroline didn't want me to, but I think you should hear about it. If you want to."

"I want to."

Bill nodded. "I thought you might. The thing of it is that Belinda had a real problem with men."

"All I know is that she got engaged a lot. But she never married."

"That's because she could never get along with anybody. Not from the time she was a little girl. She sure couldn't get along with me."

Stanley leaned forward and rested his forearms on the table. "Why not?"

"Well, for one thing, she always wanted to argue. It was almost as if she *liked* to argue."

"Lots of people like to argue."

"Not the way Belinda did. She'd take issue with anything. If you said a song had a nice melody, she'd tell you why it was boring. If you said an actor did a good job in a movie, she'd tell you why the performance was terrible. And if you weren't bothered enough by her contrariness to argue with her, she'd find something else to be contentious about."

"Sounds pretty irritating."

"It sure was. Not that Caroline and I agree on everything. I wouldn't want you to think that. But at least we agree on most things."

Stanley thought about Jane and how he and she had never had an argument of any consequence. Lots of people probably wouldn't believe that, but it was true. All those years together, and the worst disagreements they ever had were about whether to eat Chinese or Italian.

"That's not all, either," Bill said. "Belinda was a terrible gossip. No secret was safe around her. You know what Benjamin Franklin said about secrets?"

Stanley didn't know.

"It was in that *Poor Richard* thing. He said something like 'Three can keep a secret if two of them are dead.' "

Stanley laughed. "Sounds true enough."

"You bet. But in Belinda's case, if she was the one still alive, even having two of them dead wouldn't matter. Belinda would still tell."

"So you think she knew a dangerous secret? Or that she told something she shouldn't have?"

"No way to know that. But she might have. It wouldn't be the first time."

"Tell me about some of the other times."

"Well, there was the time she was dating Jim Nugent."

Stanley sat up straight. "She dated Jim?"

"Sure did. Back a long time ago. While you were up in New York."

"What happened?"

"It was when Jim was working for the regular police in Alexandria. He did that before he started his security service. You knew about that, didn't you?"

Stanley said that he'd known.

"Well, what happened was that Jim and Belinda were out on a date. Jim was off duty at the time, of course, but there was some kind of robbery at a grocery store near where they were coming out of the movie theater." Bill broke off. "After that things get a little fuzzy. Maybe I ought not to say anything. Caroline wouldn't like it."

"You know better than to try stopping now. You can't start something like that and then try to weasel out of telling it, not when Caroline isn't around to stop you."

"I guess I do know better, at that. Okay. The way I heard it was that Jim could have done something about the robbery. The guys who pulled it ran right by him and Belinda. They must've looked pretty suspicious, running down the street, waving guns around, carrying a paper sack full of money with some of it spilling out on the sidewalk."

"I think *I* would have been suspicious. What happened?"

"Nothing. At least as far as Jim was concerned. He told Belinda that it wasn't any of their business and that they'd better get out of there. Which they did. Belinda didn't want any part of it."

"But she told about it later?"

"Told everybody who'd listen. To make it worse, the two robbers got away scot-free. They never caught 'em."

"And that's when Jim left the force."

"Right. It wasn't like he was fired or anything, but that was pretty much the end of his career as a policeman. He tried a few other things, but nothing seemed to work out for him. Finally, he started up that security business. He's done all right at that."

"That was all a long time ago, like you said. Do you think Jim would hold a grudge about losing his job for that long, and then kill Belinda because of it?"

"You never know about people."

"That's the truth," Caroline said, entering the kitchen. "It's your turn to talk to Marilyn, Bill. I hope you don't fill her ears like you've been filling Stanley's."

Bill grinned at Stanley. "I'll be nice."

## 13

# The Short Good-bye

Caroline wasn't inclined to talk about either Belinda or her conversation with Marilyn. Stanley didn't have time to be irritated with her because the guests began leaving for their afternoon travels, and he wanted to remind them about that evening's supper.

"Don't worry," Mr. Brodnax told him. "We'll be back in plenty of time. After that pie we had for lunch, I'm not going to take a chance on missing a single meal that's served while I'm here."

After Stanley had seen everyone off, he was about to go back inside when Marilyn came out. Stanley supposed that she had waited discreetly so there wouldn't be any awkwardness with the guests, though he realized that she might simply have been going over her notes.

"Did you find out anything useful from Bill and Caroline?" he asked.

Marilyn shook her head. "Nothing I didn't know already. I have a lot more people to talk to now that you've given me some names."

"I hope one of them can help you. And I hope you don't think that anyone here would be involved in poisoning Belinda."

Marilyn gave him a quizzical look. "Are you trying to pump me, Stanley?"

Stanley's first impulse was to say no, but that wouldn't have been exactly the truth. So he said, "Maybe. I don't guess I'm very good at it, though."

"No, you're not. But you don't have anything to worry about. I'm sure Caroline and Bill didn't do it."

"You are?"

"Not really. I was just trying to reassure you."

"Great. Now I feel a whole lot better about everything."

Marilyn laughed. Stanley liked the sound of it. Suddenly he wanted to make her laugh again, but he couldn't think of anything to say that might do the trick. Maybe he was going to have to hire some gag writers, perish the thought. Writers were all crazy.

"A murder investigation's not the end of the

world, Stanley. I know you're taking Belinda's death personally because she was killed here at your inn, but even if one of your employees turns out to be guilty, that's no reflection on you."

"Yes, it is. Besides, Bill and Caroline are more than just employees. They're my friends."

"Everybody's your friend. Maybe you should learn not to be so trusting."

Stanley shook his head ruefully. "I think it's probably too late for me to change."

"Maybe that's good. Sometimes I think there's not enough trust around these days."

"Even in a place like Higgins?"

"Even here. You might find that out if we don't solve this crime soon."

Stanley liked to think that Higgins was immune to all the ills that beset the rest of the world, a sort of oasis of peace and quiet that hadn't changed in forty years.

"I think I'd rather not find out."

"I don't blame you." Marilyn smiled. "Well, I'd better get back to town and talk to a few of those people who were nearby when Belinda died."

"Are you going to talk to Jim Nugent?"

"He's on the list. Why?"

"Oh, no reason."

"You have a reason, Stanley."

"Well, I just thought that maybe you and Jim . . . that maybe you and he had sort of . . . well, you know."

"No, I don't know. I don't have any idea what you're talking about."

Stanley's head was getting warm, and not just because he was standing in the sun. He wished he'd learn to keep his big mouth shut.

He said, "I don't think I have any idea what I'm talking about, either. Let's just forget it."

Marilyn took her notebook out of her purse and flipped it open. She found the page she was looking for and said, "Bill told me about Jim and Belinda, but he didn't have to. I knew all about that already. Is that what's worrying you?"

"Well, I don't know much about criminal investigations. I don't know what's considered talking out of turn and what's not, so I wasn't sure whether to bring up something that far back in the past."

Stanley knew that he was skirting the issue, and he was a bit uncomfortable with the half-truth, but Marilyn didn't seem to notice.

"We never know what's important in something like this," she said. "Anything could be, no matter how insignificant it might seem to be. So if you find out anything at all, you let me know."

"But what if it's just gossip?"

"Sometimes that's the best source we have. You keep your ears open."

"I will."

"And tell me whatever you find out."

"I'll do that," Stanley said, wondering when he would get the opportunity.

Marilyn waited a few seconds, and when Stanley said nothing further, she started toward her car.

Just before she reached it, she turned and said, "I'll see you later, Stanley."

It sounded just enough like a promise to make Stanley wonder exactly what she meant.

# 14

# At the Hop

Stanley spent the rest of the afternoon puttering around the inn. He fed the goldfish, pulled some weeds in the garden, and took some time to brush Cosmo, from whom he removed enough loose hair to stuff a mattress. Not a king-size mattress, maybe, but at least a twin.

"Bill was right about you," he told the cat, who purred loudly throughout the whole process, enjoying it thoroughly. "It's a wonder you haven't choked to death."

After cleaning a thick pad of hair out of the brush for the fourth or fifth time, he put the brush on a shelf on the back porch and checked on Caroline's preparations for supper.

"Fried chicken, mashed potatoes and cream gravy, biscuits, and honey," Caroline said. "We'll start working the healthy stuff in on them tomorrow."

Stanley's mouth watered. "Honey's healthy."

"It certainly is. Good for your allergies."

Stanley didn't have any allergies, but he didn't say so. He went into the office to catch up on his bookwork, and by the time he'd finished, the Fergusons had returned. Stanley was showing them around the grounds when the Stuttses joined them. Both couples had been to Mount Vernon that afternoon.

"But the grounds there have nothing on your place," Mrs. Stutts said. "This is just lovely. I especially like the garden. Who keeps it for you?"

When Stanley said the garden was his own responsibility, everyone expressed amazement that a former television star would know anything about growing vegetables.

"I've always liked growing things," he said. "Even a weatherman has to have a hobby. When I lived in the city, I grew peppers and tomatoes in pots on my balcony. Now that I'm in the country, I'm taking advantage of owning a large piece of land. Some of the vegetables you'll be eating at the meals here come from my garden."

Stanley wasn't sure they believed him. Too many people liked to put others in little boxes and were disappointed if the boxes were the wrong size. He was supposed to be a weatherman, not a gardener.

The Stuttses and the Fergusons went back inside to get ready for supper, and Stanley went into the parlor and slipped a tape of an episode of *The Shadow* into the cassette player.

It wasn't that Stanley had anything against television. TV had been very, very good to him. But so had radio, and radio had been good to him first. It was a little like first love, he thought. You might never be able to return to it, but a lot of affection was still there. Or maybe you *could* return to it; he didn't want to rule anything out, especially not the way he was feeling about Marilyn.

At any rate, one of the reasons he'd always liked radio was that it allowed him to use his imagination. He'd always liked to think, for example, that young man-about-town Lamont Cranston looked a lot like, well, Stanley Waters. And as for Margo Lane, she probably looked quite a bit like Marilyn.

As the theme music, which for some reason Stanley remembered was "Omphale's Spinning Wheel," faded, Orson Welles began the show with his famous query: "Who knows what evil lurks in the hearts of men?"

That was a really good question, Stanley thought as he sat down to listen.

The fried chicken was even better than Stanley had thought it would be, the batter a golden brown and seasoned to perfection. There was just enough black pepper in the smooth cream gravy, which was so delicious that Mr. Jackson covered not only a huge mound of mashed potatoes with it but two of his biscuits as well.

After supper, everyone sat in the parlor while Stanley regaled them with stories about his early days in radio, even going back to his high school years when he had talked the owner of an Alexandria station into letting him do an hour-long after-school show called *Teen Sock Hop*.

Sandy Ferguson said, "I'll bet it was a really popular show."

"It was," Stanley said, false modesty not being one of his vices.

"I'd have given a lot to hear that show. Could you tell us about it?"

"I can do better than that."

Stanley located a CD with some popular songs from the mid to late 1950s and put it on the CD player. Then in his best disc jockey's voice he said, "Now here's one for all you slow dancers out there, and you know who you are. I won't mention any names, but some initials are Jerry Rhode and Nancy Whitten."

As he was saying *Whitten*, he started the CD player and the strains of "Could This Be Magic" by the Dubs filled the air.

Sandy Ferguson kicked off her Easy Spirits and dragged her husband off the couch. He looked a bit surprised, but he got over it quickly. They started two-stepping around the room. By the time the lead singer had pronounced the word *magic*, the other three couples had joined in.

Stanley watched for a second and then left the room. No one noticed him leave, which wasn't surprising. Everyone had been transported back to another time and another place.

Stanley wished Marilyn were there. They had danced to that song more than once. But she was probably out somewhere with Jim Nugent, who would no doubt have taken advantage of her questioning him to ask her for a date.

Stanley went into the kitchen, but Bill and Caroline were no longer there. They had gone to their apartment, leaving the kitchen spotless. The faint odor of fried chicken was still in the air, and Stanley opened the refrigerator to take a peek inside. Sure enough, a single drumstick was left over.

He snagged it with his right hand and went out on the back porch. There was no sign of the cats. It was getting dark, and they were probably already curled up in Stanley's bedroom, or prowling around the grounds somewhere.

The drumstick was cool but not cold, and Stanley knew it would be just as tasty as when it had been warm. He bit into it and tore off a small chunk with his teeth. As he chewed, he thought about Belinda, and then he remembered what Bill had said about the boric acid in the barn.

Might as well check it out, Stanley thought. He put the drumstick back in the refrigerator where it would be safe until he could finish it later.

The evening air was pleasantly warm, and Stanley thought he saw a couple of fireflies bouncing through the air over the goldfish pond like windblown sparks from some long-gone winter campfire. There was no sign of the cats.

An old oak tree near the barn threw a dark shadow over the door. Stanley thought for a second about going back to the inn for a flashlight, but he didn't really need one. Hal Tipton had wired the barn for electricity, and the light switch was just inside the door. The grounds were lighted as well, with the lights set to come on automatically when it got just a little darker than it was now.

As he walked toward the barn door, Stanley wished for a second that the lights had already come on. The shadow of the tree moved slightly in the faint breeze of late evening, giving the barn wall a sinister appearance.

Stanley laughed at himself. The wall didn't look any different from the way it had looked on many other evenings. Listening to *The Shadow* had stirred up his imagination too much, that and the fact that Belinda had been murdered.

The barn door was slightly ajar when Stanley got there. That was unusual. Hal was generally careful to make sure that everything was secure, and as far as Stanley knew, no one other than Hal would have any business in the barn.

Stanley reached out and touched the door. For a second he let his fingers rest on its rough wooden surface, then pushed it open. It made a noise like the door on *Inner Sanctum,* which was another radio show that Stanley listened to occasionally. The squealing of the door was a pleasantly eerie sound on radio, but it was a lot less pleasant in real life. There was some WD-40 on the shelves. Stanley decided that he would spray a little on the hinges.

"Hello?" Stanley said when the squeaking

stopped. He ran his hand along the wall, fumbling for the light switch.

He felt a little foolish for saying anything. Of course no one was in there; if there had been, the light would have been on.

Stanley reached for the light switch, but before he could locate it, something scraped on the barn floor. Stanley looked into the darkness and saw something move in the shadows.

"Who's there?" Stanley yelled, just as the shelf that stood along the wall came crashing down.

# 15

# Shadow Man

Besides boric acid and WD-40, the shelf held all kinds of things, including gardening tools, motor oil, clippers, trimmers, electrical cords, potting soil, paint, cleaning rags, and flowerpots, along with plastic boxes of nails, bolts, screws. There were also any number of household tools, most of which bounced up off the floor and banged against Stanley's shins and feet.

Hands outstretched, Stanley stumbled forward and tripped over the shelving. He fell sprawling, his face buried in a pile of oily rags, his left arm entangled in an electrical cord that writhed as if it were alive.

"Hummmmpph!" Stanley yelled.

As a cry for help, it wasn't particularly effective, and his thrashing around wasn't exactly designed to frighten off any prospective attackers.

After a short struggle, Stanley threw the cord off his arm and tried to stand up, but he could hardly move. He had fallen between two of the shelves, and he was stuck.

Great. Next the mysterious intruder would probably brain him with a hammer.

Stanley pulled the rags away from his mouth, spitting out the oily taste. He put his arms against the floor and pushed. He popped free from the shelving, rolled over on his back, scraping his backbone against the shelf in the process, and sat up.

He'd never turned on the lights, and it was now quite dark in the barn, but not so dark that he couldn't see the shadowy figure of a man approaching him. The man was carrying what looked like a large club, and he appeared ready to bash Stanley's brains out.

At least it's not a hammer, Stanley thought as he felt around on the floor for something to fight back with, not that he'd ever been particularly good at fighting. He was an innkeeper, not a brawler.

His hand closed on one of the rags that had been in his mouth. Even wadded up, the rag didn't seem likely to deter anyone, much less a man with a club, so Stanley dropped it. His fingers scrabbled around the floor until they stopped at a screwdriver.

That was more like it, except that Stanley wasn't sure that he could stab anyone with a screwdriver. He wasn't even sure that he could *threaten* to stab anyone with it.

On the other hand, he didn't want to get his brains bashed out with a club.

He stood up, holding the screwdriver out in front of him the way he'd seen someone do in a movie long, long ago. *Rebel Without a Cause*? He wasn't sure, not that it mattered.

He tried to brace his feet and kicked over a half-empty can of something or other. It clattered against the shelf.

"Stay where you are," Stanley said to the shadow. "I have a knife."

While he wouldn't tell an outright lie in ordinary circumstances, he thought it would be all right to make an exception in this case.

The shadow man had drawn back the club in preparation for his bashing, but now he lowered it.

"Stanley? Is that you?"

"Hal?" Stanley asked, lowering the screwdriver to his side with relief.

"Jeez, Stanley, you nearly gave me a heart

attack." Hal put down the club, which Stanley now realized wasn't a club at all; instead, it was a short length of two-by-four. "Do you really have a knife?"

"No. But I do have a screwdriver."

"Why don't you turn on the light? It's dark in here."

"Good idea."

Stanley stuck the screwdriver in his back pocket and turned to the wall. He located the light switch and flipped it up. The light came on and shadows danced around the walls. Almost at the same instant, the outside lights glowed to life.

"You oughtn't sneak up on a man in the dark like that," Hal said. "Scared me spitless."

"I wasn't sneaking. What were you doing out here in the barn in the dark, anyway? I didn't even know you were on the grounds."

"My car's parked right out in front of the inn. You must've come out the back way."

"That's what I did. Why didn't you stop in to see me?"

"I didn't want to intrude on your boarders. I just came by to check on the wiring, and I wanted to make sure the outside lights were working all right. I wouldn't have wanted anything to go wrong on the first day."

"Nothing's gone wrong today." Stanley looked down at the floor. "Not unless you count this mess."

"I'll clean it up tomorrow. It's not as bad as it looks. Thank goodness none of the paint cans popped open. Then we would've had a real problem."

Hal bent over and began setting up some of the cans. Stanley helped him out.

"How did the shelf happen to fall, anyway?" Stanley asked.

"Like I said, you scared me. I was reaching out to get something, and when you sneaked up on me, I must've grabbed the shelf and jerked it over."

They stood up, and Stanley said, "We should do something so it won't fall again. Could be dangerous."

Hal agreed. "I'll take care of that tomorrow, too. I'll anchor the shelves to the wall. Should've done it in the first place."

"What were you doing here in the dark? Why didn't you turn on the light?"

"Wasn't dark when I came in, and I didn't plan to stay long. I just got busy, and I could see all right. I would've turned on the light pretty soon."

"What were you looking for on the shelf?" Stanley asked, feeling a little guilty for the question.

Hal didn't seem to mind. "A pair of gloves. I was going to do a little work on one of the outside lighting fixtures, and I didn't want to scratch my hands. What were you looking for in here, Stanley?"

Although Stanley still much preferred telling the truth, he found that lying wasn't hard at all. Maybe he had a natural talent for it.

"I was just walking around the grounds. I saw the barn door open, and I thought I'd better check it out. I've been a little skittish since Belinda died."

"The word around town has it that she was murdered."

"That's the official word, too." Stanley didn't mention that Hal could expect a visit soon from Marilyn Tunney or one of her minions. "I can't imagine who would have done such a thing. Belinda never hurt anyone."

Hal shrugged. "Maybe. But lots of people didn't like Belinda much. She was nosy, and she liked to talk."

Stanley had heard that already, from Caroline and Bill. "What about you? Did you like her?"

Hal looked down at the mess on the floor and aimed a gentle kick at a half-empty tube of caulking. The tube rolled a couple of inches and bounced off a paint can.

"I dated her a time or two. But I guess you knew that. It wasn't any secret, and it didn't make me any different from a lot of guys in Higgins."

"I'd heard about it."

"Well, she wasn't easy to get along with, that's for sure. Not that she and I ever had any major fallings-out. Not like the one she and Lacy Falk had last year."

"I don't remember hearing about that."

"You must've been out of town, then. Everybody else heard about it. Belinda went out with Barry Miller a time or two, and Lacy didn't like it."

"Why not?"

"I guess Lacy thought Belinda was intruding on her territory. Lacy's been after Barry for years, ever since he came here, just about. Not that it was doing her any good."

Lacy's pursuit of Barry was well known in Higgins, and something of a joke. Barry had moved to Higgins about ten years earlier and opened M & B Antiques in partnership with Tommy Bright. He was reserved and mannerly, and he wasn't known for his enjoyment of the local nightlife, such as it was, or any nightlife at all. He kept to himself, and except for his fairly frequent buying trips he hardly ever left town.

Lacy, on the other hand, was brassy and loud. Her unisex styling salon was called Bushwhackers, a name that Stanley often wondered about. It seemed to him vaguely obscene, but maybe he just had a dirty mind. Anyway, obscene or not, Bushwhackers was always filled with loud talk and laughter, and Lacy was usually at the center of things. She was known to tip a few glasses at the local tavern when she got the chance, and in most ways she seemed quite the opposite of Barry Miller. Nevertheless, the two of them got along fairly well, and the state of their relationship was of great interest to most of the population of Higgins.

"Did Lacy say anything to Belinda about Barry?"

Hal grinned. "She didn't *say* anything. She did something."

"What?"

"She gave Belinda a bad haircut."

"That's it? A bad haircut?"

"It was a *real* bad one. Made Belinda look a lot younger than she was."

"I'd think Belinda would like that."

"It didn't make her look young in a good way. It

made her look about six years old. People laughed about it, and Belinda said she'd get even."

That sounded promising, Stanley thought, though it would have been more promising if Lacy had been the one who'd been killed.

"Did she try?"

"She sure did. She put sugar in the gas tank of Lacy's car."

"Did Lacy catch her?"

"Well, no. But she was sure Belinda did it. She got back at her, though."

"How?"

"Belinda colored her hair, but she didn't have it done at Lacy's place. She didn't want people to know she colored it, even if everybody *did* know, so she did it at home. Anyway, the next time she went in Bushwhackers for a wash and blow-dry, she insisted that Betsy Rollins do the job. Wouldn't let Lacy near her. But Lacy slipped something into the rinse water. Stripped all the color right out of Belinda's hair."

It sounded to Stanley almost as if a regular backwoods feud were going on between Lacy and Belinda.

"What happened then?"

"Belinda sued Lacy in small claims court. I

don't think anything ever came of it. Belinda probably dropped the suit. I guess they made up."

Maybe, Stanley thought, or maybe there was more to it than that. He'd have to be sure to tell Marilyn.

Hal took another look around the barn. "If you'd give me a hand, we could set up this shelf."

"Sure," Stanley said, bending down.

"Get a good grip, now."

Stanley took hold of the shelves and said, "Ready when you are."

"On three. One . two . . . three!"

On the signal, Stanley heaved upward and the shelf moved smoothly off the floor and back against the wall.

"Thanks," Hal said. "I'll be in tomorrow to clean up the rest of this."

"I'll see you then," Stanley said, walking to the door with him. "I'm going to look around in here for a minute."

"Anything special you're looking for?"

"Just checking things out. I want to make sure nothing was broken."

Stanley waited until Hal had gone before he began looking. He'd already spotted a yellow-and-black can earlier, but he'd avoided showing any interest in it. Now he picked it up.

The black letters said Roach-Be-Gone! and one of the major ingredients was boric acid. In fact, there was hardly any other ingredient. Opening the can, Stanley peered inside. About half of the Roach-Be-Gone! was missing.

Stanley inspected the can under the light and wondered if Hal had really been reaching for a pair of gloves—or if he'd come to remove the evidence of a crime.

Stanley closed the can, set it down on the floor, and went back to the inn.

When the wind's in the east,
the fishing is least.

When the wind's in the west,
the fishing is best.

Wind from the south
blows the hook in the fish's mouth.

# 16

# Haircut

"Damn, honey, I just don't think you need a haircut," Lacy Falk said, giving Stanley a professional once-over.

"I'm feeling pretty shaggy," Stanley told her, feeling that he was becoming quite an accomplished liar. He wasn't sure whether to be proud or not.

The truth was that he didn't feel shaggy at all. He'd had his horseshoe of hair clipped only the week before, to be ready for the televised activities at the inn, and it had hardly grown out at all. But he'd wanted an excuse to spend some time in Bushwhackers, and the haircut was the only thing he could come up with.

"Well, I guess we can do you, then. You'll have to wait till one of the girls is free, though."

Stanley didn't mind waiting. He'd been counting

on the fact that he'd have to wait, in spite of the WALK-INS WELCOME sign in Lacy's front window.

"I'll just sit down and read one of your magazines," he said, taking a seat in one of the metal chairs under the long mirror that lined one wall of Lacy's shop. Air squooshed out of the vinyl seat, but no one seemed to notice. It had probably happened to them, too.

There wasn't a lot of privacy in Bushwhackers. Stanley could look out the front window and see the post office across the street, the City Hall in the town square, and even a bit of the M & B Antiques storefront next to the post office. Lacy was in a great spot to see a lot of what went on downtown, which was probably why she'd chosen it, that and the fact that it was an excellent location for any business.

Across from the mirror under which Stanley waited were the chairs in which the customers sat to get their hair cut, washed, dried, teased, permed, and colored. In the back of the shop, a couple of heavy-duty dryers reminded Stanley of a more sedate version of the electric chair. He was glad that he'd never have to sit in one of them, as some woman whom Stanley didn't recognize was now doing.

Two women were seated near Stanley. He didn't

know them, either, but they appeared to know who he was. They waggled their fingers at him in a semblance of a wave, and he smiled in return. One of the women was reading a thick novel titled *The Healer's Calling,* which Stanley gathered had something to do with doctors. Or maybe it had something to do with home remedies. Stanley couldn't quite make out the cover.

Lacy and her three coworkers were busy with customers. Janet Norris had a woman bent over backward, her head in the sink, rinsing her hair and talking about something that had recently occurred on *All My Children.* Apparently Erica had been having problems with Dimitri again. Stanley gathered that it wasn't unusual.

Betsy Rollins was clipping Pearl Gray's hair with scissors, snapping her gum in time with each click, and Tammy Vaughn was blow-drying the wavy mane of Garret Young, an insurance salesman who held the policies on Blue Skies. Stanley nodded at Young and allowed himself a moment's envy of anyone who could grow so much hair.

Lacy herself was busy with a petite woman who Stanley believed must be getting some kind of hot-oil treatment. Stanley was as much a stranger to hot oil as to waving locks.

Stanley breathed in the odor of waving lotion,

hot oil, soap, and unidentifiable chemicals, then picked up a copy of *People* and began learning the fascinating details about what a number of TV and movie stars had been like before they'd become famous. He was shocked—shocked!—to discover, for example, that Jay Leno had been the class clown.

After a few minutes of heady intellectual stimulation, Stanley put the magazine down and looked at Lacy, who was talking to her customer about a sale at Victoria's Secret.

"I never go into Alexandria that I don't go by there," Lacy said. "Ever' now and then they put those panties and bras on sale, and you can buy one and get another one for half price. And I do love a bargain."

Stanley allowed himself to be momentarily distracted by the thought of Lacy in undergarments from Victoria's Secret. Lacy was nearly six feet tall, big-boned, and had enough teased blond hair to fill a hall closet. She always said that big hair was a part of her Texas heritage that she couldn't slight, no matter how long she'd lived in Virginia.

"Lord, honey," he'd heard her say once, "in Texas we start teasing our hair when we're five years old. It's part of a girl's beauty secrets."

Stanley figured that the Victoria's Secret people

were missing a bet by not using Lacy in their catalog. Maybe with a whip and a German shepherd. On the other hand, as he recalled from his one look at the catalog, Victoria's Secret generally went in for more wholesome images, and younger women, too, though Stanley thought that was a mistake. Lacy was somewhere on the shady side of forty-five, but Stanley had a feeling that she'd held up well and would show off the wares just as fetchingly as some mere stripling.

But Stanley hadn't come to Bushwhackers to mull over illustrations for catalogs. He'd come for information if he could get it.

He didn't know why exactly, but his encounter with Hal Tipton had whetted his appetite for undercover work. It was as if he'd discovered an entirely new part of himself, a part that enjoyed being sneaky and practicing deceit.

A lot of people might have been a little scared to discover that they enjoyed such things, especially after a lifelong custom of scrupulous honesty, but not Stanley. He thought of the new feeling as a healthy reaction to the fact that someone had murdered Belinda Grimsby on his property, practically right in front of him, on a day that he'd been looking forward to for so long. Stanley took it as a personal insult, and he was determined to do something about it.

Of course, he knew better than to try doing anything. He knew that he should leave everything to the professionals, to Marilyn and her police force. But he wanted to be a part of things. There was a kind of thrill in investigation that Stanley hadn't experienced in a long time, and he wanted to see if it was something that would pass or that he would enjoy for the long term.

He told himself that it wasn't that he intended to become some kind of amateur snoop and skulk around the back alleys of Higgins, Virginia, prying into everyone's private life. Far from it. He wasn't even interested in people's private lives, not unless they impinged on Belinda's. In those cases, however, he was very interested indeed, and he thought that Bushwhackers was the place to come for information.

With all that in mind, he said, "Lacy, have you heard anything about funeral arrangements for Belinda?"

The blow-dryer stopped suddenly, the scissors ceased, and Betsy even stopped chewing her gum. Only the big dryer in the back of the shop kept humming. Everyone was looking at Stanley as if he'd mooned the entire shop.

Finally Lacy said, "Hell, honey, I hear ever'-thing that's going on in this town. You know that."

Betsy started snapping her gum again. Tammy Vaughn clicked on the blow-dryer.

"Well?" Stanley said.

"Tomorrow afternoon, two o'clock, Jamar's," Lacy told Stanley, and to her customer she said, "You just keep on lyin' back, honey. I'll be done with you in just a minute."

"Are you sending flowers?" Stanley asked.

Once again it got very quiet in the shop. Stanley had to force himself not to squirm in his chair. Maybe he wasn't as good at this investigation stuff as he thought.

But Lacy didn't seem bothered. She said, "Honey, I'm sending the biggest damn arrangement you ever saw. Belinda was about as good a friend as I ever had in this town."

Betsy Rollins stifled a giggle, and Lacy turned toward her.

"Now you just cut that out, Betsy. I know Belinda and I had our little differences, but that was all in the past. I forgave her for what she did, and she forgave me."

"I'm not so sure." Betsy had a high, childlike voice that went with the gum-chewing. "I don't think she ever got over that haircut. Or that gray hair."

"Did her good to let people see her natural color," Lacy said. "I think a girl ought to let the natural color show through every now and then, just so she'll remember what's really there."

Stanley couldn't resist. "When's the last time you let yours show through?"

Lacy fixed him with a pair of hard blue eyes. "About 1984. I didn't say you should show it all the time."

"That's right," Stanley said. "You didn't."

He reached for the copy of *People,* though he wasn't interested in looking at it anymore. He just couldn't think of anything else to say, and he thought he'd already learned something anyway.

But Lacy wasn't through with him. "I loved that Belinda. She was like a sister to me."

"Yeah," Janet Norris chimed in. "I remember how my sister loved me. She used to hide behind the couch when I brought a date to the house and make noises like a dying cat."

"Speaking of cats," Lacy said.

"Don't look at me," Janet said, and smiled at Stanley.

She had a round face and a nice smile, which

Stanley thought was not marred at all by the little gap between her top front teeth.

"I'll tell you what," Lacy said. "Why don't we all get back to work. We don't have time to stand around talking. We've got people waiting."

No one had to be told twice. It was Lacy's shop, after all, and everyone knew that people were just waiting to take over a chair if Lacy ever fired anyone.

Stanley leaned back in his chair. He was pleased with himself. He was convinced that Lacy had still been feuding with Belinda, though she was trying to convince everyone that she and Belinda had been friends. But in spite of what she said, it was clear that no one really believed her. Everyone knew that Belinda's only real friend was Ellen Winston.

The woman who was reading *The Healer's Calling* said, "Mr. Waters?"

Stanley turned his head toward her. "Call me Stanley."

The woman smiled. She was about fifty and no doubt one of Lacy's good customers. Her red hair didn't match any natural color Stanley was familiar with. She closed her paperback, sticking a finger in it to hold her place.

"Stanley, then. I'm Maxie Collins."

"Pleased to meet you, Maxie."

"Me, too. I mean, I'm pleased to meet *you*." She laughed. "I saw you on TV yesterday, and there was a lot more about you and your inn on today."

Was it Stanley's imagination or had the temperature in Bushwhackers suddenly dropped ten degrees?

"Today?" he said, afraid that he knew exactly what was coming next.

"Oh, yes. All about the murder. They had tape of everything."

"Everything?"

"Oh, yes. You looked so heroic, shoving your way through the crowd to get to poor Belinda. She'd been eating salsa, they said."

"I wasn't shoving."

"Well, it certainly looked that way to me, not that I blame you, you understand. Anyway, Belinda was eating salsa, wasn't she?"

Stanley had to admit it.

"They said that Caroline made it. Is that right?"

Stanley had to admit that, too.

"Hmmmmmm," the woman hummed.

Stanley no longer wanted a haircut. He wanted to get outside and get some fresh air. He stood up.

"I'll be back in tomorrow," he told Lacy. "I have to run a little errand that I forgot about."

Lacy gave him a sickly sweet smile. "I'll bet you do, honey. Well, you come on back when you get ready, and we'll give you a little trim."

By the time she finished the sentence, Stanley was already out the door.

# 17

# He Looked So Natural

Stanley took a few deep breaths of the clear Virginia air to clear the smell of hair and hairspray out of his nose, then looked up and down the street.

People were passing by on the sidewalks on both sides, but thank goodness none of them pointed at him and yelled, "Poisoner!"

He didn't take much comfort from that because most of them were tourists. They might not even have recognized him.

Stanley took another deep breath, trying to relax and be a little less paranoid. After all, he'd expected that the media would make as much of a show of Belinda's death as they could. It wasn't as if it were something that would go on forever. In fact, by tomorrow Belinda would be forgotten and her place taken by the newest sensation of the moment, whatever it might be.

While Stanley was standing there thinking things over, Tommy Bright drove by in his completely restored 1957 Chevrolet Bel-Air, a two-door hardtop, red over white. Stanley admired it tremendously, and he'd even asked about buying it, but Tommy wouldn't consider selling. He liked the car as much as Stanley did. Maybe more.

Tommy and Barry Miller didn't sell or collect cars, exactly, but they would take what they could find at a bargain. Tommy had found the Chevy somewhere in Texas, or that was the story he told. Barry drove a 1963 MG-B, which Stanley also thought was pretty classy.

But the Chevy and the MG were their drive-to-work cars. Their business car, on the other hand, was completely different. It was a navy blue 1988 Chevrolet Nova that looked as if it hadn't been washed since its first owner had driven it off the lot. It had been in a wreck at one time or another, and the right fender was accordioned backward for a foot and a half. The windshield was cracked. The trunk lid was held down with a rope that ran from somewhere inside the trunk to somewhere underneath the body. You could hear the muffler from two blocks away.

The car was kept in deplorable condition for a purpose, of course. Barry took it on his buying trips up and down the back-country roads of Virginia and all the surrounding states. When he was trying to talk someone out of an old butter churn, he wanted to look like a poverty-stricken vagabond, not a prosperous antiques dealer.

It occurred to Stanley that anybody that sneaky might be devious enough to poison somebody.

He walked across the street to the post office, turned left, and went next door to M & B Antiques. Barry Miller met him just inside the door.

"It's just terrible about Belinda," Barry said. "I can't believe she's dead."

"She is, though," Tommy Bright said, coming in through the back door. He had a hint of a Tidewater accent, though Stanley thought he was actually from one of the Carolinas. "I've just come from Jamar's. That's Belinda they've got laid out there, all right."

"How does she look?" Barry asked.

One thing that always amazed Stanley about small towns was the fact that everyone wanted to know how dead people looked when prepared for burial. To Stanley, they generally just looked dead, but he obviously wasn't as discriminating as most people.

"She looked very nice," Tommy said. "Not at all the way she would have looked if she'd been at Lawrence's."

Nolen Lawrence owned Higgins's other funeral home, which was always second choice among the cognoscenti, for reasons that were obvious to Tommy Bright.

"Nolen always uses too much makeup," he said. "Do you remember Sara Venable?"

"I certainly do," Barry said, shaking his head. "Awful. Just awful."

"I know. I can't imagine where Nolen found that appalling shade of rouge. Poor Sara looked as if she were blushing, and you and I both know she never blushed in her life."

"I know," Barry said. Then, as if he'd just remembered that Stanley was there, he said, "But we have a customer. What can we do for you, Stanley? We have a marvelous new brass headboard right over there."

He put a hand on Stanley's shoulder and pointed. The headboard, which wasn't really a board at all, was nice all right, the brass as bright as morning, but Stanley wasn't in the market. He wasn't in the market for any of the other things he saw, either, though everything was choice. M & B held a varied accumulation of the odd, the old, and the outlandish, everything from lightning rods complete with arrows and balls to coal-oil lamps to old furniture: washstands, pie safes, china cabinets, chairs, tables, and even a fainting couch.

"I really didn't come to buy anything today," Stanley said.

"What?" Tommy said. "You mean to say that this is a social visit?"

"Not exactly. I heard that Barry used to date Belinda."

"I wouldn't say *date*," Barry said. "I did go to a movie or two with her."

"They went to revival nights at the Palace," Tommy said. "Barry's a sucker for *Casablanca* and *An Affair to Remember*."

One of Corey Gainer's more successful promotions was to have a "revival night" every Wednesday. He showed old movies that most people under the age of forty had seen only on videocassette. It might not have worked everywhere, but it was a good draw in Higgins. Stanley had been once himself, and he had wondered if he could get discount tickets for his guests. It was something he needed to talk to Gainer about.

"Corey's going to get *The Magnificent Seven* soon," Barry said. "Tommy can't resist Steve McQueen."

"Or James Coburn, for that matter," Tommy said. "Did you ever see *Our Man Flint*?"

Stanley was rapidly losing control of the conversation. To get it back, he said to Barry, "What about Lacy Falk? I thought you two were an item."

"We've been out a few times. I never took Lacy to the revivals, though, not after that time we saw *The Hustler* and she talked all the way through the film. I couldn't get her to be quiet. She kept saying over and over how young Paul Newman looked."

"Well," Tommy said, "he did."

"That's not the point," Barry said. "No one should talk in a theater, not unless it's an emergency."

"Manners have just gone to hell, haven't they?" Tommy said. "I can remember going to movies when you could actually just sit back and enjoy the show without having to listen to some old biddy sitting behind you complain about toenail fungus."

"About Belinda," Stanley said.

"That poor thing," Tommy said. "Barry only went out with her out of pity. Isn't that right, Barry?"

"Not really. I went out with her because she was good company."

That wasn't what Stanley had heard. "Someone

told me that she was awfully disagreeable, especially at movies. If you liked a performance, she was sure to hate it."

"Not true," Barry said. "Why, when we went to see *Casablanca,* she was practically in tears during the 'La Marseillaise' scene."

"That one always gets me, too," Stanley said, and then he realized that he was letting Barry distract him yet again. "But are you telling me that she never argued with you?"

"No, I wouldn't say that. I believe she did say that she thought the colorized version of *Casablanca* she saw on television was better than the black-and-white one."

"Philistine," Tommy Bright said.

"But that didn't really bother me," Barry said, ignoring his partner. "You can't expect everyone to have the same tastes."

"What did Lacy think about your dates with Belinda?" Stanley asked.

"She didn't like it much, but then it wasn't as if Lacy and I were going steady or anything. I hadn't given her my class ring."

"And he has plenty of them if he wanted to give her one," Tommy said, pointing to a glass showcase that contained, among other things, a tray of class rings from half the high schools in the state.

"Did Lacy say anything to you about your dates with Belinda?" Stanley asked.

Barry looked at the class rings as if they were the most fascinating things he'd ever seen.

"She might have said something. Or maybe not. I don't really remember."

Now I'm getting somewhere, Stanley thought. "Did she make any threats, anything like that?"

"Stanley," Tommy said, "I do believe you've been watching too many *Dragnet* reruns."

"Or *Columbo,*" Barry said. He was still looking at the rings rather than at Stanley. "What's going on here, Stanley? Have you started doing undercover work for the police?"

"Not at all. I was just curious."

"Well, then, I'm not going to satisfy your curiosity. After all, a gentleman's relationships with women aren't a proper subject for discussion."

"Hooray for a man with manners," Tommy said.

"I apologize for asking," Stanley said.

He could see he wasn't going to get anywhere with the antiques dealers. They were making things too difficult, and he wasn't a trained interrogator. Maybe he could talk to Marilyn about that, get her to give him a few pointers.

He turned as if to leave the store and then turned back. If they thought he was acting like

Columbo, he might as well give them a good reason.

"One more thing."

"Oh, my God," Tommy said. "It's Peter Falk, as I live and breathe, but without the raincoat. What can we do for you, Lieutenant?"

"Both of you were standing by the table when Belinda died, weren't you?"

"More or less," Barry said. "What about it?"

"Nothing much. I'd just like to know who else was standing near you."

Barry thought for a second. "Frankly, I don't remember."

Tommy smiled. "Me neither."

"Is that what you're going to tell Chief Tunney when she asks you the same thing?"

"Maybe," Barry said. "Or maybe not. I don't want to seem rude, Stanley, because you've been a good customer, but it's really not any of your business what we saw or didn't see that day."

"That's one way to look at it, but Belinda was murdered at my inn. I think that makes it my business. Did you see anyone near the salsa? Did you see anyone put something in it?"

"Of course not. If I had, I would have told the police immediately. I wouldn't help someone cover up a criminal act, especially a murder."

"Me neither," Tommy said.

Stanley had always liked the two antiques dealers, but he was beginning to revise his opinion. He was also beginning to wonder just exactly why they were so reluctant to talk seriously to him. It was almost as if they were hiding something.

Oh, well, he thought, if they were hiding anything, Marilyn would find it out soon enough.

"I'm sorry if I offended you, but having someone killed at my inn offends me."

"No hard feelings," Barry said. "Right, Tommy?"

"Right."

Stanley grinned. He might not have been successful in his interrogation, but at least he was going to get in the last word.

"Me neither."

# 18

# Rest in Peace?

Stanley thought that as long as he was in town, he might as well go by the funeral home and pay his respects to Belinda. It was something he had to do sooner or later.

He didn't think he'd do any more sleuthing. He was rapidly losing his enthusiasm for it. He'd begun in both Bushwhackers and M & B by thinking that he was getting some useful information, but in both places he'd wound up feeling as if some kind of joke were being played on him, though he wasn't quite sure just what the joke was. It was time to leave the detective work to Marilyn and to worry about running his inn.

He walked to the town square and cut across it, skirting the City Hall, an ugly modern glass-and-brick structure that had been built in the early 1980s when a "progressive" city council had gotten the idea that Higgins should enter the twentieth century. Fortunately for most of the other buildings in town, people had come to their senses upon seeing the result of the council's plans and become serious about preserving as many of Higgins's older structures as possible.

Not that the square was without its attractions. The shade from the ancient hickory and oak trees was cool and pleasant, and the green grass had recently been cut, scenting the midmorning air. The statues of the veterans were nice, too, even if they were occasionally streaked by passing pigeons. They gave Stanley a good feeling of being connected to the past, and that connection was another thing he liked about small towns.

Stanley believed that small towns (if you ignored mistakes like the City Hall) had a sense of history that was often lacking in cities. In a place like Higgins, you always had the feeling that you were a part of something that had been going on for a long time, hundreds of years in fact, and that would be going on for a long time after you were gone.

On the east corner opposite the square was the General Lee Hotel, managed by Ellen Winston. It had been built some years after the Civil War, and every now and then someone raised an objection to its name, just as they occasionally objected to the statue of the Confederate veteran on the square.

Stanley thought such objections were silly, though he knew he might have felt differently had he been a part of an oppressed racial minority. For him, the memory of Lee (who, after all, had never owned a slave in his life) was one that had little to do with the Civil War and a lot to do with a time when a man's word was his bond and when *duty* and *responsibility* were words that everyone understood and accepted.

And that statue of the soldier? It didn't depict a warrior; it depicted a man in a tattered uniform who carried no weapon at all. His face was weary and set, and his eyes seemed to be searching the horizon for a way home, a way back from a ravaging time of war and destruction. Wasn't everyone searching for the same thing, a way back home? Wasn't that why Stanley was in Higgins in the first place? And if he was, what was wrong with that?

Stanley walked past the facade of the hotel, glancing in through its glass doors and seeing no one in the lobby or behind the desk. He crossed the street and headed south, past Mom's Crispy

Fried Chicken (where the food wasn't at all bad, though nowhere near in the same league with Caroline's chicken), and walked down the block to Jamar's Funeral Home, which was housed in an old white house from around the same era as Stanley's inn and which had been restored with the same loving care that Stanley had used on Blue Skies.

Stanley entered through the front door and stood on the highly polished hardwood floor in the dimly lit hall. He could hear recorded organ music playing softly in the background. "Rock of ages, cleft for me . . ." Very tasteful.

The visitors' book was on a white wooden stand under a sign that announced the time of Belinda's funeral. Stanley picked up a cheap ballpoint pen that was lying on the stand and signed the book.

When he had signed, he looked around, and John Jamar materialized beside him. Jamar was about five-six and dressed impeccably in black: black suit, black shoes as shiny as the surface of a deep lake under a noonday sun, and black tie. Even the frames of his glasses were black. His shirt and pocket handkerchief were blindingly white.

"Good morning, Stanley." Jamar didn't exactly whisper, but he didn't speak out loud, either. His hushed voice didn't carry more than two feet. It was the perfect voice for a funeral director. "Are you here to see Belinda?"

Stanley nodded, and Jamar touched his arm so lightly that Stanley might have imagined it had he not seen the hand right there on his sleeve.

"She's in the Rose Chapel. Follow me."

Stanley didn't have to follow far. The Rose Chapel was just off the hallway, and several mourners were already there, sitting or kneeling in the pews. At the front of the chapel was the steel casket, covered with a smooth coat of brown paint. The silver handles reflected the lights from the ceiling.

The casket lid was open so that those who wished to do so could view the body (and no doubt comment on its condition later, as Tommy Bright had done). Sprays of bright flowers surrounded the casket, and their smell reached Stanley even where he stood.

The music switched from "Rock of Ages" to "Till There Was You." Stanley started to ask Jamar if he was really hearing a song from *The Music Man,* but then thought better of it. Maybe there was a new trend in funeral-home music that Stanley wasn't aware of.

"Would you like to see Belinda?" Jamar asked.

*Not really,* Stanley thought, but he was sure that

wouldn't be the right thing to say, either. So he said, "Yes."

Jamar touched him lightly on the arm again as if to urge him on, and Stanley started down the aisle, wishing he'd dressed a little better for the occasion, not that Belinda would mind. He didn't recognize any of the mourners until he got nearly to the first row of pews and Ellen Winston looked up at him from where she knelt.

She didn't look good. Her hair was tangled, as if she hadn't combed it since the day of Belinda's death, and her eyes were red. She wasn't wearing makeup, either, and she looked much older than her years. Deep lines were etched in her face, running downward from the corners of her mouth.

Stanley felt sorry for her, and he started to say something, but Ellen beat him to it.

"This is all your fault," she said, putting her hand on the railing in front of her and pushing herself up.

She was clutching a tattered tissue in her hand. She dabbed at her eyes with it and then crumpled it into a ball in her fist. Stanley thought for a second that she might throw it at him.

"Your fault," Ellen said again, her voice breaking.

Stanley felt terribly self-conscious. He knew

that no matter how intent the other mourners had been in their grief when he had entered the chapel, they were now all thinking of him and wondering if Ellen was right.

Ellen stepped up so close to Stanley that she was practically touching him. He could feel her hot breath when she spoke.

"You came here where nobody wanted you after you lost your job, and you built your little monument to the past, and this is what happened!"

She pointed dramatically toward the casket, while Stanley stood there feeling like the biggest fool in Higgins, VA. He didn't know what to say, a condition that was becoming all too familiar to him lately.

"I don't think this is the right place to get into a discussion of my inn," he said finally.

"Your inn! This town didn't need any inn. It had a perfectly good hotel already. But you didn't care. All you cared about was finding some way to get attention now that you couldn't be on television every day."

"I could be on television if I wanted to," Stanley said, feeling more like a fool than ever. Why was he defending himself to this emotionally disturbed woman?

"And now look what you've done," Ellen went on as if he hadn't spoken. "You've killed Belinda."

Stanley opened his mouth, but no words came out. He knew that there were people all over New York City who wouldn't believe such a thing was possible, but it was. John Jamar materialized at his side again.

"Now, Ellen," Jamar said, reaching out to put a hand on her arm.

"Belinda was a lovely person, but he poisoned her like a roach," Ellen said, jumping back from Jamar as if his hand were the flattened head of a striking snake.

The backs of her legs struck the edge of the pew, and her knees buckled. She put out a hand to catch herself, but she grabbed only air. She fell to the floor and rolled halfway under the pew.

Jamar bent over to help her up, but she refused to take his hand. She twisted away from him and lay there sobbing.

Some people—maybe most people—would have lost their composure in such a situation, but not Jamar. Stanley assumed that the funeral director had seen just about everything during his career and that the sight of a weeping, practically hysterical woman lying under the pew of the chapel was nothing that he couldn't deal with.

Stanley, on the other hand, couldn't deal with it well at all. "Should we call a doctor?"

"No, no, it's just grief. Mourning takes all kinds of forms. She'll be all right."

Jamar knelt down on the floor beside Ellen, who had now rolled over on her stomach. The sounds of her sobbing wrung Stanley's heart. He knew what it was like to lose your best friend. It had happened to him when Jane died, and for months he had felt like crawling into some dark hole and hiding from the world.

Jamar whispered something to Ellen that Stanley couldn't hear, and the intensity of her sobbing seemed to lessen slightly. After a few more seconds, she got control of herself and allowed Jamar to help her to her feet and out of the chapel by way of a door to the side of the altar.

Stanley didn't follow them. He was certain Ellen didn't have anything more to say to him, not anything he wanted to hear, anyway, and he no longer felt like paying his respects to Belinda. Without even a glance into the open casket, he walked back down the aisle, past the mourners, who were pretending to have not the slightest interest in him but who were all watching him out of the corners of their eyes.

He wondered how many of them actually

thought he'd killed Belinda. Probably more than one of them.

He told himself that it didn't matter, that Marilyn didn't think he'd had a thing to do with it.

But he wondered if that was really true. What if Ellen had talked to Marilyn? What if she'd convinced Marilyn that Stanley was guilty?

Never happen, Stanley thought.

Will it?

# 19

# Unfriendly Conversation

Stanley walked back to where he'd parked his car, a black Lexus ES 300, in the lot behind the old Baptist church on the corner across the street from Bushwhackers. Stanley had been baptized in the church as a child, and since he'd returned to Higgins, he had been attending it more Sundays than not. He figured his fairly regular attendance gave him a right to use the parking lot occasionally.

The Reverend Mr. Turner was changing the marquee on the sign out front, putting up the title of his sermon for the coming Sunday: "How Shall It Profit a Man?"

"Good morning, Preacher," Stanley said.

He'd never felt comfortable calling ministers by their first name, as so many people did these days, but then he didn't feel comfortable calling them *Mr.* either, since so many of them were younger than he was and seemed embarrassed by the formality. So he'd solved the problem by calling them *preacher*. It seemed to work all right.

The Reverend Mr. Turner, a small, neat man in his workaday jeans and blue shirt, looked around and said, "Good morning, Stanley. That was a terrible thing about Belinda."

Stanley agreed that it was. "Will you be conducting her funeral service?"

"Yes. Tomorrow at two o'clock. Her sister asked me, though Belinda hasn't been to church for years and I don't know her very well."

Turner had been the pastor for only five years and was thus regarded by all the old-timers as a rank newcomer in Higgins. For that matter, the old-timers thought of just about anyone not actually born in Higgins as a newcomer. Even Stanley wasn't entirely accepted. He might have been born there, but he hadn't lived there all his life.

"What about the graveside services?" Stanley asked.

"In the old Higgins cemetery," Turner said, to distinguish Belinda's final resting place from the new Higgins cemetery, which had been opened only a few years previously when the city hadn't been able to obtain any more property in the vicinity of the old cemetery. "Her parents are buried there, and they bought Belinda a plot years ago when they bought their own."

It was almost as if they'd known that their daughter would never leave Higgins and never marry. Stanley thought that was almost as sad as Belinda's death. He went on to his car, leaving the Reverend Mr. Turner to put up the scripture and to close up the glass front of the sign.

As Stanley drove back to the inn, he thought about Belinda and about her sad life. He wondered if anything in her past might have made her so quarrelsome, and then he thought about Jim Nugent.

Jim had seemed singularly undisturbed by Belinda's death for a man who had once dated her. Though Stanley didn't have a wide dating experience, it seemed to him that a man would retain at least some feeling for a woman he'd been out with. He wouldn't have dated her if he hadn't liked her, would he?

Of course Jim might have been soured by what had happened. Belinda was at least indirectly responsible for his leaving the police force, and that could account for his indifference, even if it didn't really make him a suspect.

Or did it?

Stanley found himself getting interested in

sleuthing again, even after his earlier failures, and he turned the car down a tree-lined street, circled a block, and headed out of town. It wasn't far to Alexandria, and Stanley had always enjoyed the drive, since he avoided the main roads and lazed along through the green countryside. That way, he was more likely to see cows than billboards, and that was the way he preferred it.

It was nearly noon when Stanley pulled into a parking spot near the entrance to J & N Security. Nugent's car was right in front of the door, so Stanley knew that Nugent was probably in the office.

An indescribable electronic noise sounded when Stanley opened the door, but no one was in the room, which looked to Stanley a lot like a doctor's waiting room. A worn beige carpet was on the floor, and several matching chairs were scattered around the room. Old fishing and hunting magazines lay on a coffee table that sat between two chairs.

Nugent came out of a door in the middle of the back wall. He was dressed in his uniform, and he seemed surprised to see Stanley, which was understandable. Stanley didn't really have any reason for being there.

Nugent didn't look glad to see Stanley, either, which was odd. Stanley thought they had parted friends.

"Hello, Stanley. What can I do for you? Got any more grand openings coming up?"

"I hope not. At least not if they're like the last one."

"I wouldn't worry about that. We don't have a lot of poisonings around here."

"I wanted to ask you about that. Before Belinda died, did you see anybody standing around who might have slipped the poison into the salsa?"

"If we're going to talk about that, we'd better go in my office." Nugent turned and went back through the door without looking to see if Stanley was following.

The office surprised Stanley. The walls were decorated with framed stills of western-movie stars: Clint Eastwood in *Fistful of Dollars,* John Wayne in *Hondo,* Paul Newman in *The Left-Handed Gun,* Marlon Brando in *One-Eyed Jacks.*

"I didn't know you liked westerns."

"Yeah. My heroes have always been cowboys." Nugent closed the door. He walked behind a cheap imitation-oak desk and sat down, frowning at Stanley. "Now what was it that you wanted to know?"

Stanley sat in what he assumed was the client's chair. He'd hired Nugent over the phone for the opening.

"I wondered who you saw standing near the table when Belinda was poisoned."

Nugent leaned back in his chair. "Funny you should ask. Marilyn Tunney wanted to know the same thing. And she has a good reason. She's the police."

"So she's already been here."

"Not that it's any of your business, but the answer is yes. Early this morning, in fact. She knows how to do her job, Stanley. She doesn't need you waddling around behind her to check up."

Stanley sighed inwardly. That bit about waddling was entirely uncalled for. So was the rest of Nugent's statement for that matter. But Stanley didn't say so, because the truth was that he wasn't checking up on whether Marilyn was doing her job. That wasn't really his purpose at all.

What he really wanted to know now was whether Nugent had asked Marilyn for a date, but he couldn't ask that. He had to stick with his original question.

"I know she doesn't need me to help. But I'm curious. Belinda was killed on my property, after all, and I have a right to know who did it."

"There are plenty of possibilities," Nugent said with a nasty smile. "In fact, you're one of them."

"Did Marilyn say that?"

"Anything I said to her is confidential. I think you'd better leave now, Stanley. I'm getting a little bored with our conversation."

Stanley didn't move. "You used to date Belinda, a long time ago, but you didn't seem very upset when she died."

"Like you say, it was a long time ago. People change. I've changed, Stanley, and so have you. I remember you when you were just a kid. With hair. And now you're a big-time former TV star. Who would ever have guessed?"

Stanley thought the remark about the hair was a real cheap shot, and he didn't much like the use of *former*, but he let it pass. He was having trouble deciding why Nugent had become so hostile.

"You should still care about her a little."

"Do you care about the girls you dated when you were a kid? Can you even remember all their names?"

"Not all of them," Stanley admitted, thinking that it was true even though there hadn't been that many.

"See what I mean? Belinda was so far back in my past that it seems like a different person dated her. And I only went out with her a couple of times, anyway. Go on home, Stanley. Leave the investigating to the real police."

Stanley kept right on sitting in the chair. "You're probably right. But you were standing right there by the table just before Belinda died. Surely you saw some of the people who were there."

"What I saw or didn't see isn't any of your business. But I think I've told you that once already, haven't I? You don't have a badge, you don't have a gun, and you don't have any authority. So just forget about going around asking questions. You don't know how to do it."

"Maybe not, but I have a right. A private citizen can ask as many questions as he wants to ask. I may not have a badge, but I know that much."

Stanley wasn't going to mention to Nugent that Marilyn had told him to ask questions. Nugent probably wouldn't believe him, anyway.

"You can ask, but nobody has to answer. At least *I* don't have to answer. So long, Stanley."

Nugent opened a desk drawer and pulled out a copy of *Outdoor Life* and began flipping through the pages. Stanley watched him for a few seconds, but Nugent didn't look up.

After a few seconds of silence, Stanley stood up and left.

# 20

# Who, Me?

It was midafternoon when Stanley got back to the inn. All the guests had left early in the morning with plans to spend the day in Washington. Stanley had planned for Caroline to pack lunches when the guests wouldn't be at the inn for a meal, but only the Fergusons had taken advantage of the offer. The others said that they'd find a restaurant.

Stanley himself was hungry, but he didn't want to eat too much and spoil his supper. He checked the refrigerator and discovered that the fried chicken was gone. Bill must have eaten it for lunch. He settled for a ham sandwich and a glass of iced tea.

After eating, he went upstairs to check on the rooms. Bill had done his job perfectly. The beds were made, the floors gleamed, the bathrooms were spotless. Later, maybe Stanley would ask if the Fergusons had used the chamber pot.

He went back downstairs to look over his books and see who would be checking out and who would be arriving within the next several days. He didn't get much done, however, before the doorbell rang.

He was pleased to see that his visitor was Marilyn Tunney, or he was pleased until he got a good look at her expression, which wasn't exactly one of delight.

He welcomed her to the inn, and she said, "Stanley, what have you been up to?"

"Uh," Stanley said, horrified to discover that now he was reduced to speaking in grunts, which he thought was even worse than saying nothing at all.

"Don't *uh* me, Stanley Waters. You know what I'm talking about."

"Uh."

Marilyn gave him an exasperated look. "I told you not to do that. Aren't you even going to ask me in?"

Stanley recovered his voice. "Sure. Would you like to come in?"

"I'm not sure. But I suppose I will."

Stanley opened the door wider and stood to one

side. Marilyn walked past him and kept right on going until she was in the parlor. Stanley trailed along behind.

Marilyn sat on the couch and said, "You've really been causing trouble in town, Stanley."

Stanley sat on the couch, but not too close to Marilyn. He wouldn't want her to get the wrong idea.

"You told me to ask questions."

"Ha. So it's all my fault, right?"

"I'm not sure. What are we talking about?"

"The first thing we're talking about is Ellen Winston practically killing herself in a fall at Jamar's chapel. John's afraid she might sue."

"That wasn't my fault."

"Right. I wish I had a dollar for every time I've heard that one."

"This time it's the truth." Stanley went on to tell her what had happened.

"That's not exactly the way Ellen tells it. She wants to have you arrested for assault."

"There were witnesses. John, for one."

"I know, and they all told me pretty much the same story you did. Which means that you won't have to spend the night in jail, at least not tonight. That won't make Ellen very happy, I'm afraid."

"Would it help if I called her? I could tell her I was sorry."

"I don't think it would help a bit. In fact, I don't think she'd appreciate hearing your dulcet tones in the least. But let's forget Ellen for a minute and talk about Barry Miller and Tommy Bright. What did you do to them?"

"Not a thing. I just visited their store. Don't tell me they want me arrested, too."

"They didn't say anything about arresting you, but they aren't exactly fond of you. *Busybody* was about the nicest word they used."

"I don't know what could have upset them. Unless they have something to hide. In fact, they sounded like they *might* be hiding something."

Marilyn didn't appear interested in whether Barry and Tommy were hiding anything. "There's more. You caused a disturbance in Bushwhackers, too."

Stanley tried to look innocently surprised, but he didn't think that he succeeded very well.

"Me?"

Marilyn didn't smile. "You. And you didn't stop there. You even drove over to Alexandria."

"I didn't create a disturbance in Alexandria, though," Stanley said self-righteously.

"No, but Jim wasn't exactly pleased when you

showed up and started asking questions like you were Peter Gunn."

Stanley almost laughed aloud. He hadn't thought of Peter Gunn in thirty years. Or more. What a great name! And then he started thinking how great it would be if Bushwhackers were owned by Peter Gunn. He could almost see the sign painted on the big glass window: PETER GUNN'S BUSHWHACKERS.

"I don't see what you think is so funny about all this."

Stanley straightened his face. "Nothing. Not a single thing."

Marilyn wasn't fooled. "Stanley, somehow I don't think you're cut out to be a detective."

"Don't you want me to tell you what I found out?"

"You didn't find out anything, did you?"

"Yes, I did. I found out that Jim Nugent is acting pretty strangely. His attitude toward me has changed completely since Belinda died. And I found out that Barry and Tommy are hiding something, or they act like they are. And Lacy Falk's not telling the complete truth, either. She even tried to convince me that she and Belinda were the best of friends."

"Okay," Marilyn said, giving him a thoughtful

look. "Maybe I was a little hasty. Maybe you have found out a few things. Why don't you tell me more?"

This was more like it. Stanley relaxed for the first time since Marilyn had come in. He leaned back against the couch and told her everything.

"Stanley, you amaze me," Marilyn said when he was finished.

"I did good, huh?"

"Well, I wouldn't say *that*. But you actually didn't do too badly. For an amateur. It's just that you didn't really find out anything. We're talking facts here, not opinions. We can't arrest somebody on the strength of an opinion."

"I know that."

"Oh, don't look so hurt. If nothing else, you did stir things up a little. It might seem surprising, but most people don't really get nervous when the police question them. It's something they expect. But when someone like you comes blundering in, it throws everything off. People do strange things."

"Like roll around under chapel pews."

"Not that. That wasn't so strange. Ellen was emotional, and then she fell down. After that she was embarrassed and upset. Who wouldn't be?

What's strange is that you managed to make so many people act guilty."

Stanley didn't know whether to feel proud of himself or not. Making people feel guilty didn't seem like a skill that would be in much demand.

"So what does that tell us?" he asked.

"What does *what* tell us?"

"That everyone's acting guilty. What does that tell us?"

"How should I know?"

"Well, you're a cop. Aren't you?"

Marilyn finally gave Stanley a smile. "That doesn't mean I know everything, I don't have any more idea of what's going on than you do."'

Stanley found that pretty hard to believe. He had absolutely no clue as to what was happening.

"Could it be that everyone's guilty?" he asked. "I saw a movie once where it turned out that everyone—and there were quite a few people involved—was guilty."

"That might work all right in the movies, but it never happens like that in real life."

Stanley found himself getting interested. It occurred to him for the first time that he didn't know a lot about real life, not when it came to murder. Most of his information came from movies and television.

In fact, Belinda was the only person he knew who had ever been murdered. He had known people who died in accidents, and of course he'd known quite a few who'd died of natural causes. But murder was something entirely outside his experience. If he was really interested in getting to know Marilyn better, and if murder was a part of her life, maybe it was time he learned something more about it.

"How does it happen in real life?" he asked.

"Well, we really don't have that many murders in Higgins. But I've studied the subject quite a bit, and it's pretty much the same everywhere."

"That doesn't help me a whole lot. I haven't been around murder a whole lot."

"I can believe it. Okay. Here's the deal. When someone is killed, there are always three things involved: a motive, a means, and an opportunity. In Belinda's case, we've established the means. Poison. Now we have to establish the motive and the opportunity."

"Which is why we're trying to find out who might have been standing near the table."

"Right. And finding out the motive wouldn't hurt. In fact, that's crucial."

"What if everyone has a motive?"

Marilyn sighed. "Don't start that again. In real

life, murder is committed by individuals, not by groups, unless the group happens to be a gang. And the good news is that we don't have any gangs in Higgins. Yet."

"In the movie, it was individuals. They were acting separately."

"Forget the movie, Stanley. It's not going to be like that."

"I don't see why not. Lacy won't talk, Jim won't talk, Barry and Tommy won't talk. Something's going on. It's a conspiracy of silence."

Marilyn laughed. "Spare me the clichés, Stanley. Most murders in what we're calling 'real life' are committed by people for two reasons—love and money."

"So we're looking for someone who could get money if Belinda died?"

"Sure. And it would be nice if whoever it was could be placed at that table."

"What about love?"

Stanley was thinking about Jim Nugent, but Marilyn took it another way.

"Bill had access to that salsa, all right. And Hal Tipton was near the table."

"How do you know?"

"He told me."

Rainbow in the morning,
sailor take warning.

Thunder in the morning
means rain before night.

The louder the frogs,
the more it will rain.

# 21

# Motive, Means, and Opportunity

Stanley heard a little inner voice saying, "Tell her about last night."

He thought about it for several seconds before deciding not to say anything. Hal might have been behaving a little strangely, but that didn't make him any different from anyone else involved in the murder.

Except for Bill and Caroline, he told himself. They were sailing along just as if nothing at all had happened. It was nice to know that some people could just get on with their lives even when everyone else was being weird.

Finally Stanley said, "What did Hal tell you?"

Marilyn settled herself as if to get more comfortable on the couch. Her movement brought her a little closer to Stanley, who wondered for just a moment if the movement was intentional. It hadn't been, of course. He knew that. Didn't he?

"Hal said that he was standing right by the table when Bill put the salsa on it, and that Bill didn't put anything in the bowl."

"See, I knew Bill was innocent."

"He could have put something in it before he ever got to the table."

"Right. But he didn't. Bill wouldn't poison anyone. Anyway, what about Hal?"

"Bill's his alibi. He says that Hal might have been nearby, though he didn't see him. Which Hal says means that he wasn't close enough to have put anything in the bowl. He could have done it after Bill left, though."

"Hal was right about one thing."

"What's that?"

"You really don't trust anyone."

"I still trust you, Stanley. No matter what anyone says."

Stanley felt as if a mouse wearing ice bags on its little feet were scampering up his backbone.

"Did someone accuse me?"

Marilyn nodded. "Just about everyone. Lacy Falk. Ellen Winston. Barry and Tommy."

"What about Jim Nugent?"

"He didn't actually accuse you."

"Gee, that was nice of him."

"Yes, Jim's a nice guy."

Stanley didn't like hearing her say that, and he didn't like himself for not liking it. He hadn't experienced jealousy for a long time, and it wasn't an experience he enjoyed.

"He's got nice hair."

"Hair's not everything, Stanley. And we're getting off the subject."

"Right. So everyone accused me, but you didn't believe them."

"Well, they didn't have any facts to back up their accusations. Just speculation and opinion."

"Like me," Stanley said, getting the point.

Or maybe not. Marilyn said, "No, Stanley, not like you."

"What makes them any different?"

"They haven't been out asking questions all over town the way you have. And you're not acting guilty like most of them are."

"So are they guilty?"

"I told you: I don't know. You can't expect normal behavior when murder is involved."

Stanley was depressed. "So what you're saying is that basically we don't know squat."

"Elegantly put."

Stanley started to say something, then realized

what he'd said: "*We* don't know squat." And Marilyn hadn't made any objection to his use of the pronoun. The little mouse cruised his spine again, but for a different reason this time.

"Would you say that we're working together on this case, Marilyn?"

"No, I wouldn't say that, but I did ask for your help. Some people aren't too fond of that idea, but I take the full responsibility."

"Who's not fond of the idea?"

"Officer Kunkel for one."

"It figures."

"But don't worry about him. Remember, I'm the chief."

"All right, Chief. If you really want my help, I've got a suggestion."

"Let's hear it."

"There's still someone we haven't talked to."

"Corey Gainer."

"Right. So I guess you've talked to him after all."

"No. I was too busy following up all the phone calls I got about you poking your nose where it didn't belong."

"But you're not mad about that anymore."

"No. I wasn't really mad in the first place, but I *was* a little irritated. Now that you've explained yourself, though, I can see that you're not really guilty of anything, no matter what people thought about you."

"I'm glad you feel that way. Do you want me to continue asking questions?"

"I guess it wouldn't hurt. So far you haven't actually caused any real damage."

"Thanks for the vote of confidence."

Marilyn gave him a nudge with her elbow. "You really wear your feelings on your sleeve, Stanley. I didn't remember your being that way."

"Usually I'm not. I think it has something to do with you."

"I'll take that as a compliment."

"That's the way it was intended." Stanley felt the top of his head begin to warm up. "So, where does all this leave us?"

"All what?"

Stanley wished Marilyn wouldn't say things that might be interpreted two ways. His head was getting very red, and he brushed his hand across it.

"All this questioning. And all this talk about motives and means and opportunities."

"It leaves us pretty much where we started. And here's something else we have to consider. We haven't gotten the lab report yet, so we still don't actually know that the poison was in just the salsa."

Stanley thought of something. "What about the poison? Do you have any idea where it might have come from?"

"Kunkel's checking on that. He's not having much luck, though. Boric acid is fairly easy to come by."

Stanley remembered the can in his barn, but he didn't say anything about it. He didn't want to get into that just yet, if ever.

"What about Corey Gainer? Are you going to talk to him?"

"Of course. Even if you beat me to it. I have to talk to everyone."

"Speaking of that . . ."

"Speaking of what?"

"Of your talking to everyone. It's just occurred to me that I've told you everything about my conversations, but you haven't told me a single thing about yours. Well, except that everyone would like to see me drawn and quartered on the town square at high noon. What did *you* find out?"

"I'd like to tell you, Stanley, but I can't."

"Why not?"

"Because what you found out is just talk. What I found out is part of an official police investigation."

"But you told me about Hal," Stanley protested.

"That's different. I was just telling you where he said he was located. That's not confidential."

"What about the way people felt about me. Couldn't you have kept that a secret, too?"

"No. I wanted you to know. I thought it might help you the next time you asked questions. Maybe you wouldn't be quite so offensive." Marilyn saw the look on Stanley's face and said, "I mean that in the best possible way, Stanley."

Stanley was pretty sure Marilyn was going to tell him anything she wanted him to hear and keep the rest to herself. He didn't blame her for that, however. He was keeping some things back from her, after all.

He would never have guessed that deception could be so easy, though he supposed that Marilyn was probably used to it. As a cop, it was something that she most likely encountered all the time. He thought about asking her, but he didn't think it would be wise. She might have asked him about deception in the world of television, where it was supposed to be common, but the truth was that Stanley had rarely experienced it and had never indulged in it. He thought that Marilyn might have a hard time believing that.

So he just said, "I'll try to be less offensive from now on. So what about Corey Gainer?"

"Can't you think of a way to approach him?"

As a matter of fact, Stanley could. "This is Wednesday. Why don't we take in the movie tonight?"

"Why, Stanley, I thought you'd never ask."

Me, too, Stanley thought.

# 22

# Stepping Out

For Stanley, the rest of the afternoon went by with approximately the speed of the last ice age. Glaciers formed and melted. One-celled animals emerged from the slime and evolved into sentient creatures.

He tried to make the time pass faster by working in his garden, but he couldn't concentrate. After he chopped up a tomato plant instead of a weed, he put his hoe away and walked down to the creek. Even the rippling sound of the water didn't do much to calm him.

He wondered what had come over him. He was hardly a ladies' man, and he hadn't intended to get involved with a woman, much less a woman who appeared quite ready to encourage his involvement.

He thought about the rest of his conversation

with Marilyn, but he found he couldn't remember much about it. He was sure she had told him that she'd be quite pleased to go to the movie with him, in an unofficial capacity of course, and if the opportunity arose for Stanley to question Corey Gainer, in an unofficial capacity of course, well, that was just fine with Marilyn. But she didn't care. She was just glad to be going to the movie with Stanley.

Or that was what he thought she'd said. He hoped he wasn't just making it up. To top it all off, he didn't even know what the movie was. It was "classic" night, however, so he knew that whatever the movie was, it would be good.

The guests began to arrive back at the inn in the late afternoon, and Stanley busied himself with greeting them and asking about their trips to the capital. They were full of stories about all they'd seen, and all of them planned to make another visit the next day. The ones who had missed the Smithsonian just had to see it, while the ones who'd been there wanted to visit the monuments.

Stanley wondered why they hadn't just stayed later in the city rather than make another trip. Then it became clear to him: the food. No one who ate one of Caroline's meals was going to eat restaurant food any more than necessary. They had lean center-cut pork chops, okra and tomatoes, corn on the cob, peas, and biscuits. Dessert was a rich chocolate pudding with whipped cream and a cherry on top.

Health food, Stanley thought. You can't beat it.

The guests seemed to agree. After eating, they sat back in their chairs with the blissful expressions of religious seekers who had experienced visions of the divine.

While Bill was cleaning up the kitchen, Stanley talked with the guests in the parlor for a short time. He was glad that they'd had a big day and were planning for another one tomorrow. That meant they all wanted to get to bed early, which fit right in with Stanley's plans.

He put a tape of *I Love a Mystery* in the cassette player and told everyone to enjoy it, that he'd see them in the morning. And then he was off to get ready for his date.

He showered, shaved close, and even put a dab of Brylcreem on his hair. Well, less than a dab. Maybe half a dab. A full dab was overkill in his case. There was nothing to comb, after all. He just wanted to give what hair there was a little shine. As he finished dressing, Bill knocked at the door. Stanley told him to come on in.

"What's going on?" Bill asked, giving Stanley the once-over. "You have plans for the evening?"

Stanley told him that he was going out to a movie.

"All by yourself?"

"Not exactly. I'm going with Chief Tunney."

Bill didn't look anywhere nearly as happy about that as Stanley was.

"Chief Tunney, huh? I didn't know you two were such good friends."

"We've known each other for a long time, off and on. It's not like it's a date or anything." Stanley said it with a straight face. It wasn't really a lie. He didn't know whether it was a date or not.

"You going to buy her some popcorn?"

Stanley hadn't planned that far ahead. "Maybe."

"It's a date then," Bill said, and that settled it. "You'd better be careful, though. She's a cop, and she might be setting you up."

"Setting me up? How?"

"For a fall. She asked me a lot about you yesterday."

The excitement that Stanley had been feeling for most of the day lessened considerably. He felt his heart settle in his chest.

"What did she ask?"

"Oh, whether you were in the kitchen when

Caroline was making the salsa, things like that. She's a suspicious woman, Stanley, and she's a cop. I think you might be forgetting that part."

Stanley tried not to let his disappointment show on his face, but he wasn't much of an actor. Doing the weather hadn't required that he be a thespian.

"I understand that it's her job to be suspicious," he said without much conviction.

"It sure is. That's why I'm telling you to watch what you say to her."

"I didn't kill Belinda, Bill. Why should I watch what I say?"

Bill shrugged. "Just a word to the wise. Have fun at the movie."

"I'll try," Stanley said, knowing it wasn't going to be anywhere near as much fun now as he'd hoped.

The plan was for Stanley to meet Marilyn at the theater, which, like nearly everything in downtown Higgins, was just off the town square. It was a block to the east of Bushwhackers, a block to the north of the General Lee Hotel.

And it was next door to the city jail.

When he was a kid, Stanley had sometimes wondered what might happen if there should be a jailbreak in the middle of a movie. He had imagined the frenzied pursuit through the theater of prisoners resembling the Three Stooges and dressed like the Beagle Boys in a Scrooge McDuck story. The cops all looked like Frank Lovejoy, wearing snap-brim hats and carrying movie-issue .38-caliber revolvers.

In his little fantasy, Stanley saw moviegoers climbing over seats and crawling under them, while he, Stanley Waters, unflinchingly heroic eight-year-old, captured the escapees by threatening them with his Red Ryder BB gun. His parents could never understand why he wanted to take the BB gun to the movie with him, he recalled, but it had made perfect sense to him. You could never tell when it might come in handy.

Nowadays things were different. The cops, some of them anyway, looked like Marilyn Tunney, and Stanley was sure that no prisoners would escape during the movie. And Stanley no longer owned his BB gun. He didn't own any guns at all, and in fact he didn't like them. His theory was that guns were dangerous in the wrong hands, and sometimes even in the right hands.

In most ways, all three changes were good, but they did take some of the excitement out of going to a picture show.

Stanley parked on the street in front of the furniture store next to the theater, locked his car, and walked back to the Palace. The theater had been built sometime in the 1930s, and Stanley considered it a miracle that it had survived both the advent of television and the invention of the VCR.

Actually, it almost hadn't. It had been closed for several years in the 1970s; it had been used as a church for a few years after that, and then it had been closed again until Corey Gainer had come to town in the early 1980s. By all accounts he was a movie buff who had inherited enough money to live comfortably and who didn't have to worry if he didn't make a huge profit with the theater.

In that way, he was a little like Stanley with his inn. For Gainer, the theater was a labor of love. He was doing something he liked to do, and making people happy at the same time. Stanley liked him and certainly hoped he wasn't guilty of killing Belinda.

Stanley turned the corner and saw the marquee. It jutted out from the front of the theater like a giant *V* lit up from within, and it was topped by a tower outlined in blue and red neon that stretched above the roof of the building.

The evening's feature was spelled out in black capital letters: *GUNGA DIN*, one of Stanley's favorite movies, with Cary Grant, Victor McLaglen,

Douglas Fairbanks, Jr., and Sam Jaffe. Stanley knew that the print would be as perfect as it could be. For his Wednesday features, Gainer showed fully restored prints whenever possible.

Marilyn was standing under the marquee waiting for Stanley, and for just a fraction of a second he felt sixteen again. Or he thought he did. He hadn't been sixteen in so long that he wasn't sure. At any rate he was filled with a mixture of apprehension and exhilaration that was somehow strange and utterly familiar at the same time.

Marilyn looked toward him and smiled, and Stanley forgot all his misgivings and Bill's warning. Or if he remembered them, he didn't care. He walked to Marilyn and said, "Hi."

"Hi, yourself." She pointed up at the marquee. "Have you ever seen this movie before?"

"Only about a hundred times. Why?"

"I think it has an interesting subtext, that's all."

Stanley didn't get it. "Subtext? What's a subtext?"

"It's something we big-time movie intellectuals like to talk about, that's what."

"Great. That helps me a lot."

Marilyn laughed. "Let's just say that there's a story going on beneath the story that the writers thought they were telling."

"Thanks. That clears it right up for me."

Marilyn hooked her arm through his and guided him to the ticket booth, which hadn't changed a bit since the theater was built. The prices had, however. Instead of ten cents, Stanley paid six dollars for each ticket. He collected them from the ticket-seller, who was so young that she probably had no idea who Victor McLaglen was, and escorted Marilyn inside.

"Now about that subtext," he said as they went through the wide double doors.

"Forget it. Let's just enjoy the movie."

"Sounds good to me." Stanley handed the tickets to Corey Gainer, who took up the tickets only on Wednesdays. "How are you tonight, Corey?"

"Doing fine," Gainer said, though he didn't sound as if he meant it. He averted his eyes and didn't look at either Stanley or Marilyn.

Gainer was a stout man who liked to dress like Sydney Greenstreet, at least on Wednesdays. He wore an old white suit, and he even had a white hat, though he didn't wear the hat inside the theater.

He made a feeble joke. "You two enjoy the movie, but no holding hands. I don't allow that."

"We'll watch ourselves," Marilyn said.

Stanley felt his head heating up. To cover his

embarrassment, he asked Marilyn, "Want some popcorn?"

"Sure. It smells great, doesn't it?"

Stanley nodded. He figured that Corey popped the corn in coconut oil. No wonder it smelled so good.

They went over to the concession counter, and Stanley bought a red-and-white-striped bag of popcorn and two Cokes. On Wednesdays, Gainer charged much less for the treats, though he hadn't gone so far as to charge prices from forty years ago. The popcorn was a mere fifty cents.

They went inside the darkened theater and took seats near the rear. Stanley remembered sitting in the front row when he was a kid, but his eyes had changed since then.

"We didn't do a very good job of interrogation," Marilyn said as they settled into their seats.

"We'll get him later. Trust me."

"I do. Remember?"

"Oh, yeah," Stanley said, hoping that she really did.

# 23

# Where's Corey?

Stanley thoroughly enjoyed the movie, just as he had every single time he'd seen it. The fact that he was watching it with Marilyn only made it better, and he didn't worry at all about the subtext, even though he thought he caught on to what she was saying. "It has something to do with male friendship, doesn't it?"

"Very good, Stanley. All the really good movie love stories seem to be about men and other men instead of men and other women."

"For example?"

"You mean besides *Gunga Din*?"

"Right. Besides that."

"How about *Butch Cassidy and the Sundance Kid*?"

"That's one."

"Not to mention *The Sting, The Defiant Ones*, and *Beau Geste*, just to pick a few at random."

"What about *Thelma and Louise*?" Stanley asked.

"Touché. I was only kidding, anyway."

"I thought so."

They were standing in the lobby as the other moviegoers filed out. Most of them gave Marilyn and Stanley a wave and a smile.

"Where's Corey?" Stanley said, looking around.

Marilyn looked, too. No one was working in the lobby except a teenage girl behind the concession counter. She was bagging all the leftover popcorn and standing the bags in the back of the popping machine.

"Maybe he's inside, cleaning up," Stanley suggested.

"I don't think so. He has someone else to do that."

"Okay. He's outside then."

"That's possible, but he hardly ever goes outside. On Wednesdays, he's always in the lobby to greet people as they leave and ask them how they liked the movie."

"That's right," Stanley agreed, remembering his previous visit to the theater. "I wonder what happened to him."

"Could it have been us, do you think?"

Bill's warning about Marilyn's suspicious nature returned full force to Stanley. But he also remembered that the way Gainer had behaved when they entered the theater was enough to make anyone a mite distrustful.

"Could be," Stanley said. "Where do you think he is?"

"Let's check his office." Marilyn led the way to a brown-painted door that was beside the entrance to the ticket booth.

She knocked on the door. There was a hollow echo, but no other response. She tried the knob. "Locked."

Stanley was about to ask if she was going to kick down the door like John Wayne when the girl behind the concession counter called out, "If you're looking for Mr. Gainer, he went home right after the movie started. He said he wasn't feeling very well."

Stanley found that interesting. He looked quizzically at Marilyn.

"It could happen," she said.

"Why don't we drive by his house? We could pay him a sympathy call."

"We could, but he might really be sick. Why don't we get a malt instead?"

Stanley thought about the chocolate pudding he'd had for supper. He thought about the whipped cream and the cherry. "I think I'll have a diet soda instead. But you can have a malt if you want one."

"I do. Let's go."

Higgins had a downtown drugstore that Stanley regarded as a national treasure because it still had a soda fountain. The fountain didn't make much money, but it was another local labor of love like the theater and the inn.

The drugstore had been closed for even longer than the movie theater because no one had any use for the building until a young pharmacist named Raymond Grove came to town. He'd heard about the drugstore from someone who'd once lived in Higgins, and he'd been interested in opening it if the fountain could be restored.

As it turned out, it could. Grove put in a new store that was modern in all respects, except for the fountain. He hired and trained local high schoolers as soda jerks, and they made the best fountain drinks and malts in the world, or so Stanley firmly believed.

The drugstore was next door to Bushwhackers and across the street from M & B Antiques, and thus just a short walk from the theater. The evening air was cool and sweet. Stanley could still smell the fresh-cut grass of the square, and when he looked up, he saw a sprinkling of stars overhead. It seemed only natural to take Marilyn's hand as they walked along, and she made no objection. She didn't say a thing, but she gave Stanley's hand a little squeeze that he felt all the way down to the ends of his big toes.

When they crossed the street at the post office, Stanley noticed that the lights were on in Bushwhackers. He and Marilyn looked in through the front window and saw that Lacy Falk was giving Barry Miller an after-hours haircut.

"Why don't we stop in and say hello?" Stanley said.

"Good idea."

Stanley walked up to the door and knocked on the glass front.

Lacy looked over and motioned him to come in. Barry Miller didn't look too happy to see either him or Marilyn, but Lacy was enthusiastic enough.

"Damn, honey," she said to Stanley, waving a pair of trimming scissors as she spoke, "I didn't know you were dating. Are you going steady or playing the field? Has a working girl got a chance with you?"

"I'm a working girl," Marilyn said.

"Yeah, I know that, honey, but I was talking about *me*."

"Just a minute, here," Barry said from his chair.

"Don't worry, honey," Lacy told him. "I was just teasin'." Then to Stanley she said, "Where you two been?"

Stanley told her that they'd been to see *Gunga Din*.

"A wonderful movie," Barry said. "I'll give you a nickel if you can tell me who the female lead is."

Stanley, who thought he knew everything about the movie, had to consider for a minute before he said, "Joan Fontaine."

"Right. I'll have to owe you the nickel, though. I seem to have left my change in my other pants. I really thought I'd win. Hardly anyone remembers her. It's the men who stand out."

"Subtext," Stanley said.

"How astute!" Barry said. "It's a great love story, but there are no women involved."

"Sounds boring as hell to me," Lacy said. "How was Corey doing?"

"Now that you mention it, he disappeared," Marilyn said. "According to one of his workers he got ill and had to go home early."

"I'll just bet he did," Lacy said, as if she knew something they didn't.

"What do you mean by that?" Stanley asked.

"It's Belinda. That's what I mean."

Stanley started to say something, but Marilyn beat him to it. "What about Belinda?"

"Well, I never like to talk out of turn," Lacy said, trying to look pious.

"Isn't it the truth," Barry said. "Not a single word of gossip has ever tainted the sacred air within these hallowed walls."

Lacy laughed loud and long. "Damn, honey, you ought not to say things like that. You'll give me an asthma attack."

"You can tell us," Stanley assured her. "What have you heard?"

"Well, someone that works in Wirt Wallace's office came in today and talked out of turn, I guess you could say. It's probably confidential information."

Wirt Wallace was a lawyer who had an office only a couple of blocks away. He'd done the title work when Stanley bought the inn.

"If it's confidential, we'll keep it that way," Stanley promised.

That was good enough for Lacy. "Well, honey, it seems that Corey is about to come into some more money."

"What does that have to do with Belinda?" Marilyn asked.

"Just about everything. Turns out, Corey's her heir."

# 24

# A Key Point

For the first time since he'd gotten involved with Marilyn and the investigation, Stanley thought there had been a real breakthrough. They'd found a motive, and it was a motive for someone who had had an opportunity.

That is, they'd found a motive if Lacy was telling the truth and if her informant was correct.

"Did anyone say why Corey happens to be inheriting Belinda's estate?" Marilyn asked.

"Sure enough." Lacy gave Barry a pat on the shoulder and began trimming his hair using a comb and scissors.

"Well?" Stanley said.

Lacy lifted an eyebrow. "Oh, you mean you want to know why?"

Marilyn lifted an eyebrow. "It might help."

"Well, did you all ever wonder what Corey was doing in Higgins, Virginia?"

"He was running his theater," Stanley said.

"Sure he was. But what was he doing here in the first place?"

Stanley couldn't answer that one, but that was all right. Lacy answered it for him.

"Turns out that Belinda was his cousin. They didn't get along all that well, and they didn't have much to do with one another after he got here, but she's the one that told him about the Palace. They were at some family reunion or something, and she just happened to mention it. Anyway, that's the story I heard."

"Who did you hear it from?" Stanley asked.

"From Belinda."

"Oh," Stanley said. "Your good friend."

"That's right."

"And it's all very interesting," Marilyn said. "Too bad that the money, what there is of it, couldn't have gone to someone who needs it."

Stanley had to admire her technique, and it worked just as she must have intended.

"Corey needed it, all right." Lacy tapped Barry on the head with the comb. "Be still, honey. You're going to make me cut a gap in that pretty hair of yours."

Barry had twisted to look at her. "You're getting into the area of pure speculation," he said. "You don't know a thing about Mr. Gainer's affairs."

"His financial affairs or the other kind?" Lacy said, and laughed. "I can tell you a little about both of 'em."

"Right now I'm interested in the money," Stanley said. "I thought Corey was pretty well set."

"That's what I heard when he came here," Lacy agreed. "But from what I hear, that movie-theater business of his has turned out to be a mighty expensive hobby. He had to put in new air-conditioning this year, and that meant he had to have the whole place rewired. And you remember that big rainstorm the hurricane blew in here last summer?"

Stanley remembered. It had been a flood of near biblical proportions, and he was afraid at the time that the inn was in danger. Luckily he was on the high end of town.

"Well, it did some pretty heavy damage to the Palace, and all that had to be fixed up. Corey didn't have flood insurance. That doesn't come with your regular insurance, you know. You have to pay extra for it, and a lot of folks never think to ask about it. I guess Corey was one of 'em."

"From one businessman to another," Barry said

to Stanley, "I can tell you that little things like that add up. I, of course, had flood insurance, because I plan for things like that, but my store hardly flooded at all. The theater's floor slopes downward, and that's what caused some of the trouble there."

"Anyway," Lacy said, "it sort of all makes you wonder, doesn't it?"

"Wonder about what?" Stanley asked.

"Oh, nothing. Except that now that Belinda's dead, Corey won't have to worry about money anymore. She was pretty well fixed, you know. Her daddy made a fortune in real estate before he retired."

It made Stanley wonder, all right, and when he and Marilyn went next door to the drugstore, he said, "What did you think about all that?"

"I think it's something I should look into. If it's true, it certainly gives Corey Gainer a motive in Belinda's death."

"Exactly what I was thinking."

"Store's closing in fifteen minutes, everybody," said the young man behind the soda fountain. "Can I get you something before then?"

Marilyn wanted a chocolate malt, and Stanley's good intentions evaporated.

"I'll have a vanilla Coke," he said, thinking that at least he wasn't having ice cream.

He and Marilyn sat on the high stools in front of the counter and watched the soda jerk at work. He was pretty good, Stanley thought, flipping the ice cream from the scoop into the glass with an admirable aplomb. He had to move the glass only about an inch to avoid disaster.

"Should we go by Corey's house?" Stanley asked Marilyn after they'd finished their drinks.

"I'll go by tomorrow."

Stanley could take a hint: amateurs butt out. But that was all right. He understood.

"I'll just pay for these drinks," he said.

When they got back to the theater, Stanley asked if he could drive Marilyn home.

"I'll go on over to the jail," she said. "I have to check on things there before I go home. I had a very nice time, Stanley."

"I'm glad. Maybe we could do it again."

"I hope so."

There was an awkward pause. Stanley didn't know what to do, but Marilyn did. She stood on tiptoe and give him a quick peck on the cheek.

"Good night, Stanley," she said, then turned and walked away.

Stanley watched her go, a goofy smile on his face. After a few seconds, he went to his car, where his rush of happiness disappeared instantly. He was horrified to see a long silver line scratched from the taillight to the headlight in the smooth black finish on the driver's side.

Stanley wasn't a man who prided himself on his possessions. To him, a car was only a car, but the deliberate act of vandalism outraged him. He didn't even get in the car. He turned on his heel and practically ran to the jail.

The police station was on the first floor of the jail, and the dispatcher, Geraldine Calloway, stopped Stanley just as he entered. Geraldine handled the front desk on the evening shift and kept track of Higgins's three squad cars. She was stout and her uniform fit her like the skin on a wiener. She looked tough enough to chew up nails and spit out carpet tacks.

"Hey, Mr. Waters," she said. "Are you looking for the chief?"

Stanley was surprised that Geraldine Calloway seemed to know something about Stanley and Marilyn.

"I want to report a crime."

"You're kidding me, right?"

"No. I wish I were, but I'm not. Someone vandalized my car."

"What's all the ruckus?" Marilyn asked, emerging from an office near the back of the room. "Stanley? What are you yelling about?"

Stanley hadn't realized he was yelling. "Someone keyed my car."

"Huh?" Geraldine said.

"Keyed my car. You know. Ran a key along the side and scraped the paint off."

"When?" Marilyn asked.

"While we were in the movie or maybe at the drugstore," Stanley said, not caring that Geraldine was grinning at him like a possum eating pokeberries.

"I'll walk over with you and have a look at it," Marilyn said. "I'll see *you* tomorrow, Geraldine."

"Yes, ma'am." Geraldine was no longer grinning. Or not quite so broadly, anyway.

Marilyn walked past Stanley and out the door. She was walking so fast that he had trouble keeping up with her, though her legs were much shorter than his.

"What's the hurry?" he asked.

"When there's a crime, the Higgins police are on the job."

"Oh. Right."

# 25

# In the Pines, in the Pines

Stanley was still steamed as he drove home. He was so angry that he hardly glanced at the dusty car that was parked on the last side street before he reached his acreage. There was no reason for him to study the car; it wasn't unusual for cars to be parked on the streets of Higgins.

Marilyn had looked at the scratch on Stanley's car and told him that not much could be done about it. Random acts of vandalism were practically never tied to anyone. "I can write up a report. That will help you with the insurance company. You do have insurance, don't you?"

"Of course. I'm not like Corey Gainer."

"Good. Because we're never going to find out who did this."

"You really know how to inspire confidence in a

guy. Don't the cops always get their man? Or woman?"

"That's the Mounties. And as a matter of fact, I'm not so sure about them. Anyway I'm just telling you the truth. I wouldn't want to lie to you."

"I hope you're a little more confident in your murder investigations."

"That's different. Motive, means, and opportunity, remember?"

"Why wouldn't that apply here?"

"Because anyone in Higgins could have done this."

"Motive?"

"Someone hates you."

"Hates me?"

"Either that or someone doesn't like fancy cars. Or someone just saw a chance to have a little fun."

"I don't know whose idea of fun this would be."

"Me, neither. We don't have a lot of vandalism in Higgins."

"Didn't you say the same thing about murder?"

"Probably. Strange things are happening here since you moved back."

Stanley was hurt. "I hope you don't think I'm to blame."

Marilyn smiled. "Want to come back to the station and watch me write the report?"

"No thanks."

When he parked his car at Blue Skies, Stanley got out and looked around. His inn looked beautiful to him in the moonlight, and he was glad someone had attacked his car instead of Blue Skies. He didn't know what he would do if anyone tried to hurt his inn.

As he walked toward the front door, he thought he saw a light moving in the pines down by the creek.

Why on earth would one of his guests be poking around down by the creek at this time of night? All of them were supposed to be in their rooms, asleep.

Stanley remembered the half-glimpsed car. What if someone had parked on the street and slipped down to the creek?

Then he remembered the couple that had been caught skinny-dipping down there during his opening gala. It was a warm night, and maybe their romantic impulses had returned.

Stanley thought about the way Marilyn's hand had felt in his, and he wondered what it would be like to go skinny-dipping with Marilyn. The top of his head started getting warm. It was practically steaming within seconds.

Stanley knew that it would be a far, far better thing to turn his thoughts elsewhere, so he looked back to where he had seen the moving light. Maybe he should go down there and have a look, see what was going on, if anything.

He walked across the grass of the front lawn and strode toward the creek. The faint hooting of an owl sounded somewhere in the pines.

"I wonder if Hal's come back for something?" Stanley said aloud. The sound of his voice was not exactly reassuring to him, and he wondered if maybe going down to the creek alone was a bad idea.

But he didn't turn back. He was, after all, the unflinchingly brave Stanley Waters, who could take on a theater full of jailbreakers with his Red Ryder BB gun.

He wished he had the BB gun now. It would be more of a comfort to him than the stupid owl that was still hooting down among the pines.

When Stanley walked into the trees, it immediately became considerably darker, though still not too dark to see. The pine needles slid under his feet, and he heard the ripple of the creek over slick stones. He unaccountably thought of another song about pine trees that his mother had sung in her high, clear voice on occasions when she was feeling lonesome or blue:

*In the pines, in the pines*
*Where the sun never shines,*
*And I shiver when the cold winds blow . . .*

That song was even more mournful than the one about the Blue Ridge Mountains, and Stanley shivered among the pines, though there was only a light, warm breeze that stirred the tree branches above him.

Stanley peered around. As far as he could see, no one was near the stream except him. And the owl. He couldn't forget the owl.

He walked past the springhouse. It wasn't much more than a concrete trough with a roof over it, built right over the spot where a little spring trickled out of the ground. The cold spring water ran through the trough on its way to the stream and cooled the milk or butter that sat in it, though nothing was in it now. Stanley was going to begin using it soon, keeping watermelons in it as well, but he wasn't quite ready yet.

He wasn't going to be ready for longer than he'd thought, either, judging from the condition of the springhouse. Someone had done something to the roof. Stanley wasn't quite sure what; it appeared in the darkness that it had somehow been pulled off and kicked around. Considering the construction of the springhouse, that was about all the damage that could be done to it short of using dynamite.

As Stanley contemplated the damage, trying in some way to connect it to what had happened to his car, he heard a noise up near the barn.

Thinking immediately of the smokehouse, he began to run in that direction. The smokehouse was much more vulnerable to abuse than the springhouse had been.

It was a wood-frame building modeled on the smokehouse that Stanley's grandfather had built at his farm. There were two floors. The top floor was sort of like an attic and wasn't really used for anything until after the hams had been smoked and cured. Then they were stored there. But the bottom floor was where all the action was.

An enormous brick fireplace was on the bottom floor for smoking the hams. Stanley shuddered to think what someone could do to that fireplace with a few blows from a sledgehammer. For that matter, the walls certainly wouldn't stand up to any pounding, either. And a fire anywhere other than the fireplace was simply unthinkable.

It wasn't that the smokehouse would be so terribly hard to replace. It wouldn't even be expensive. But Stanley felt even more protective toward it than he did toward the inn. He hadn't seen to the building of the inn as he had the building of the smokehouse.

Stanley saw a red flickering inside the smokehouse. He ran faster.

The door of the smokehouse was open when Stanley got there. He hurled himself inside and saw that a small fire was burning in the fireplace. Smoke curled out into the room.

Who would have laid the fire? And why?

Stanley looked to his left and right. Shadows danced on the walls, but nothing else moved.

Nothing else, that is, until something scraped on the floor behind him.

Stanley started to turn, but it was too late.

Something hard and solid hit him in the back of the head, and he fell to the floor. He got his hands down to break his fall, but they didn't help. He thought he felt his nose crunch just before he blacked out.

When a cow thumps her ribs with an angry tail,
be on the watch for lightning and hail.

A ring around the moon
means that rain will follow soon.

A rooster's crow at night
calls rain for the next day.

# 26
# Conflagration

Stanley forced his way through the raging flames and slammed at the closed door with his fire ax. With each blow of the ax, the yowling from the other side of the wall became louder.

"Don't worry, Binky!" Stanley yelled. "I'm coming!"

"Meeyoorrrrrr!"

Stanley hammered at the wall. The smoke from the fire filled his nostrils. He began coughing, taking deep, racking breaths.

The coughing woke him up. He was still lying on the floor, and his nose hurt. So did the back of his head.

"Meeyoorrrrrr!" Binky said, sinking his claws into Stanley's calf.

"Ee-yow!" Stanley answered.

He sat up more quickly than he would have

thought possible. It made his head hurt even worse.

"Binky?" he said, putting out a hand to touch the cat. The smoke stung his eyes. "What are you doing here? I thought you were part of the dream."

Binky coughed.

"Okay. You're not part of the dream. Or maybe you are. I'm not dreaming now, am I?"

"Meowr?"

"Right. We've got to get out of here."

Stanley stood up. It wasn't an improvement. The room was thick with smoke.

"Put out the fire. That's the first thing."

Binky didn't say anything, since he apparently didn't have any ideas about how to go about putting the fire out. Stanley stepped over toward the fireplace, where the fire still burned. The smoke was thicker over there, and Stanley wished he had a bucket of water.

He didn't, of course. But he had his feet, and he kicked the fire apart. Sparks jumped into the smoke and glowed brightly before they vanished.

Stanley coughed and bent down to look for Binky, but he couldn't find him.

"The door," Stanley said, turning and staggering off in the direction he thought was the right one.

"Meeoorrrrrrr!" Binky screamed when Stanley stepped on him.

"Sorry, Binky. Where's the door?"

Either Binky didn't know or didn't want to say. He scuttled away and remained silent.

Stanley's hands hit the door. It was a simple door, without even a doorknob. There was an old-fashioned string-pull lift-latch.

Stanley located the string, hiked the latch, then shoved on the door. It didn't open.

He shoved harder. Nothing happened. It was as if the simple wooden door had become as heavy and solid as the vault door at the Higgins National Bank. Heavier, even.

Stanley shoved and coughed, coughed and shoved. The door didn't budge.

"Help!" Stanley yelled.

His voice rasped through his throat like a coarse metal file. He wasn't going to be able to take the smoke much longer. Neither was Binky, though at least Binky was closer to the floor and therefore not inhaling as much smoke as Stanley was.

No one answered his call.

Rubbing at his smarting eyes, Stanley remembered something he'd said to Marilyn about kicking in the door. He'd never kicked in a door before, and he didn't think he knew the proper technique. On the other hand, how hard could it be?

He raised his foot to the level of his belt and kicked straight out. He was standing too far from the door for the kick to be effective. His boot barely touched the wood, and Stanley almost lost his balance.

Tears were running down his cheeks as he stepped closer to the door and tried again. This time he was more successful. His foot hit the door solidly, jarring his body. The shock hurt both the back of his head and his nose, which was either running or bleeding. Stanley didn't much care which. If he didn't get out of the smokehouse quickly, it wasn't going to matter.

He kicked at the door again. This time he stood closer and hit it solidly. He heard and felt the crack of the wood.

Binky rubbed against Stanley's left foot. "Meowr?"

"One more time and we're out, Binky."

Then he slammed his foot into the wood once more. The door splintered right down the middle. A final kick and the opening was clear. Smoke poured outside. Stanley nudged the hesitant Binky through the doorway and followed him out.

Once outside, Binky went streaking off into the night. Stanley, on the other hand, didn't feel like streaking anywhere. He sank down onto the damp grass and breathed gallons of the sweet night air into his ravaged throat.

Stanley wasn't sure how long he sat there. Ten or fifteen minutes at least. Even then he didn't leap to his feet. He turned toward the smokehouse and crawled toward the door, looking for something that he knew would be there.

He found it easily, a short, stout stick of firewood that someone had used to prop the door shut. He started to pick it up, but then he thought about fingerprints. Would fingerprints show up on the rough surface of the wood? He didn't know, but he didn't want to take any chances. So he left the wood lying where it was.

He put up a hand and gingerly touched his nose. It was tender, and it was bleeding, but he didn't think it was broken. He tried to wiggle it. That hurt even more. But the cartilage seemed intact.

He blinked his eyes. It was almost as if someone had poured sand under his eyelids. He blinked rapidly several times, which helped, but only a little.

After a few minutes, he got up and went to the inn, proud that after the first few steps his knees hardly wobbled at all. He entered the inn through the back door. Binky came tearing up just before the door closed and squeezed himself through the narrow opening. Ignoring Stanley, he dropped his head into his food dish, gobbling up the last crumbs of diet cat food.

"You could have waited and used the cat door," Stanley said, his voice still hoarse and his throat still raspy.

There was no answer from Binky except a steady chewing noise.

Well, they're supposed to have nine lives, Stanley thought. Maybe there was something to it.

Stanley left Binky, who seemed just fine, and went into his room. Sheba and Cosmo were lying in their beds, sleeping soundly. Cosmo was snoring.

"A fine pair of watch cats you two are," Stanley said, keeping his voice low. He didn't want to disturb them. "If I left it up to you, the whole place could burn down."

Stanley moved into his bathroom and looked at

himself in the mirror. His face was streaked with soot, and his eyes were rimmed with red.

"I look like a vampire."

He'd sometimes considered acting, and he wondered if any good parts were available in vampire movies. He bared his teeth at the mirror. Pretty scary, he thought, but it would be better if he filed them to a point. But forget that. He didn't really want to be an actor that much. His croaking voice was good, though.

He pulled a tissue from a pop-up box and pressed it under his nose with his right hand. With his left, he reached behind his head and felt the knot that had formed there. It wasn't a big knot, probably not as large as a golf ball, but it hurt just the same. The skin wasn't broken, however, and Stanley was grateful for that. He didn't like the idea of having stitches.

He thought about concussions and wondered if he had one. He held up two fingers.

"Two. I must be okay."

He took the tissue away from his nose and looked at it. It was darkly stained with red. He got up and pulled a fresh tissue from the box. After he had held it to his nose for a while, he looked at it. There was a much smaller stain. Stanley figured that was a good sign.

Stanley sat on his bed and watched the cats sleep for a few minutes. Watching cats always soothed him for some reason, and he needed soothing. Either that or five or six martinis, and he didn't feel like mixing any drinks at the moment. After a few minutes Binky came in, got into his own bed, and began the tedious licking of various portions of his anatomy over and over as if nothing had ever happened.

"We smell like smoked hams," Stanley told Binky, who looked at him briefly as if to say, "Speak for yourself, fella," and then resumed his licking.

By the time Binky had completed his grooming to his satisfaction, Stanley was feeling a little better. He thought it might be a good idea to call Marilyn.

He tried the police station first, but she had already left for home. And Geraldine Calloway didn't want to give him Marilyn's home number.

"If you've got a problem, you report it to me. I'll see that it's handled right."

"I'd rather talk to the chief."

"Of course you would. But we don't believe in giving special treatment to any citizen, not even if they're dating the chief. Besides, how do I know you're who you say you are? You don't sound much like Stanley Waters."

Stanley had to admit that she had a point. He sounded like someone doing a bad impression of Bill Clinton with a mild case of bronchitis. He apologized for bothering Geraldine and started to hang up.

"Hey, wait a minute. What about your complaint?"

"Forget it." Stanley cradled the phone.

Marilyn's number was listed, of course, so Stanley gave her a call.

"Hi," she said when Stanley told her who he was. "Is this an obscene phone call or is your voice changing?"

"Neither one."

"So you just called to say you had a good time tonight?"

"Not that, either."

"What, then?"

"Well, I think somebody just tried to kill me."

# 27

# Memories Are Made of This

It didn't take Marilyn long to get to the inn after Stanley had told her his story.

"I don't usually investigate things like this on my own," she told him as they walked toward the creek.

Stanley was glad she hadn't brought Kunkel along, but he said, "I thought the department didn't give special treatment to any citizen."

He'd washed his face and cleaned up his nose. The water had helped his eyes, but the back of his head still hurt, and so did his nose.

"You've been talking to Geraldine Calloway, haven't you?"

Stanley admitted that he had. "I called the station first. But don't get me wrong. If you want to give me special treatment, that's all right by me. I won't tell anyone."

He enjoyed being with Marilyn even under the circumstances. The pines scented the night air, and even the smoky odor of Stanley's clothes was almost pleasant. The owl was no longer hooting, but a night bird was calling somewhere, and Stanley could hear little frogs chirping near the creek.

Marilyn shone her flashlight at the springhouse, which didn't look any better than it had the last time Stanley had seen it.

"More vandalism," Marilyn said. "Like your car."

"Yes. But the smokehouse thing was a lot more serious."

"Why don't we walk up there?"

They followed the yellow glow of the flashlight up to the barn, and Stanley pointed out the log that had been wedged against the door. "Do you think it might have fingerprints on it?"

"Maybe, but probably not. I don't think I've ever been involved in a case that was solved by the use of fingerprints, anyway. But I'll take it with me when I leave."

They looked at the smokehouse itself, but other than the door there was no real damage. And there was no sign that anyone had been there other than Stanley.

"Too bad Binky can't talk," Stanley said. "Maybe he could give us a description."

"Cats have brains the size of walnuts. Or maybe those marbles like the ones we used to play Chinese checkers with. I don't think we can count on Binky for any help."

Stanley's nose and head began to throb with pain. "Do you have something against cats?"

"Not really. They shed a lot, don't they?"

Stanley thought of Cosmo. "Some of them do. But you get used to it."

"Maybe. Tell me more about that car you saw when you were coming home."

Stanley was glad to change the subject. He didn't want to think Marilyn might not like cats.

He thought about the car he'd seen and wished he'd taken a better look, but it was too late now. How was he to know that someone would be lying in wait for him?

"It was just a car," he said, but then something occurred to him. "There was something familiar about it, though."

"What?"

Stanley tried to remember. He was sure he'd noticed something, but for the life of him, he couldn't remember what it was. He remembered something else, however, and he decided that maybe the time had come to tell Marilyn about it.

"I've been meaning to tell you about something that happened last night."

"Oh?" Marilyn said. "And what's that?"

Stanley told her about his encounter with Hal in the barn.

"And there's boric acid in there?"

"There's a pesticide that's pretty full of it. But that doesn't really prove anything, does it?"

"Nothing at all. But it's suspicious. You say there was no reason for him to be here?"

Stanley told her what Hal had said.

"Pretty flimsy excuse."

"But it could be true. And why would he be after the boric acid, anyway? He could have moved it anytime at all. He didn't have to sneak back at night."

"Who knows why he wanted to move it, or even if he did? He might have been there for the reason he said. His being there is at least a little suspicious, though. You have to admit that."

Stanley admitted it, but said, "I don't think that was Hal's car I saw earlier."

"It could have been anyone's car. It could have been someone who was visiting in the neighborhood. It's not as if you're isolated out here. If it was

Hal who hit you, he would have hidden his car out of sight."

She was right about someone visiting in the neighborhood. Though Stanley had several acres of land, he was well within the city limits and only a few blocks from one of Higgins's residential areas.

And she was right about Hal. He would know plenty of places that he could park so that his car wouldn't be seen.

Stanley admitted as much to Marilyn. "But there was something about that car . . . I just wish I could think what it was."

"Maybe you'll think of it tomorrow. Let's get that piece of wood."

While Marilyn was collecting the wood, Stanley thought about Hal. Would he be capable of murder? Stanley didn't think so, but then he couldn't think of anyone who would be.

"Stanley. Look at this." Marilyn was shining her flashlight on the log. "I think that whoever hit you used this chunk of wood."

She showed Stanley something that might have been blood, and maybe a hair or two. Stanley's hand went automatically to the back of his head.

"I'm glad he didn't hit me any harder, then. He could have killed me with that thing."

"I'm not sure he wanted to kill you. Maybe just scare you."

"I hope you're right," Stanley said, thinking that Hal wouldn't have wanted to kill him. On the other hand, he couldn't believe that Hal would even want to hit him.

"I'll send this off to the lab, but I don't think we'll find out anything. I wish you could remember what it is that bothers you about that car you saw."

"So do I."

"Well, if you think of it, you can give me a call in the morning. But not too early. I know that you like to get up with the chickens."

"How do you know that?" asked Stanley, thinking that it might be a good idea to get some chickens for the inn. He liked the idea of fresh eggs, and he even liked the idea of hearing a rooster crow at the crack of dawn. He wasn't so sure that his guests would share his enthusiasm for the rooster, however, though he was certain they'd like the eggs.

"I'm a cop, Stanley. It's my job to know things about people."

"So I'm just a part of your job?"

"I didn't say that."

"Well, you sort of said that."

"I also happen to remember that you were an early riser even when we were in high school. Do you remember that time you came by my house at five o'clock in the morning and threw the rock against my window?"

Stanley was taken by surprise. He hadn't thought about that morning for nearly forty years.

"Except that it wasn't your window," he remembered.

"That's right. I think my father wanted to kill you."

Stanley was laughing now. "It wouldn't have been so bad if I'd just used a smaller rock."

"I'm not so sure. My father didn't like to be woken up that early, even by someone who hadn't broken one of his bedroom windows."

"Anyway, he couldn't catch me," Stanley said, thinking about how he had ridden his J. C. Higgins bike at breakneck speed through the cool early-morning darkness, his knees pumping as the pedals whirled around. In some ways it seemed as if it had happened so long ago that it might as well have been in a different lifetime. In other ways, it seemed more like ten minutes ago.

"I was in a lot better shape in those days," he said.

"You're not in such bad shape now, Stanley. Don't underrate yourself."

Stanley patted his waistline, which would never again shrink to the circumference of his youth. He wondered what his belt size had been then. Twenty-eight? Thirty? Something like that. It had been many inches ago, and though he'd lost quite a few pounds since his early TV days, he still wouldn't qualify as skinny.

"I walk every morning," he said. "Maybe I should jog, instead."

"I wouldn't if I were you. You're fine just the way you are."

Stanley felt awkward and wished he could think of something nice to say to Marilyn. He had never been good at compliments.

Marilyn seemed to read his mind. "You don't have to say anything. I know how you feel."

"You do?"

"I'm a cop, remember." She hefted the piece of wood. "I'll let you know how this tests out, Stanley. And you can call me anytime."

"I will," Stanley said, feeling the top of his head.

He hoped it wasn't glowing in the dark.

# 28

# Late-Night Notes

Stanley sat in his desk chair and looked at the cats. As if aware of Stanley's gaze, Cosmo woke up, stretched, and turned around. Orange hairs separated themselves from his coat and wafted upward.

"Meowr," Cosmo said, considering Stanley with half-closed green eyes.

"Go back to sleep. And stop shedding like that."

Cosmo blinked, kneaded his bedding until it was satisfactory, and settled down. Neither of the other cats stirred.

Stanley examined Cosmo's head. It was awfully small. There was no way a walnut could fit inside it. A marble, maybe. Was that such a derogatory thought? Stanley had heard that humans didn't use nearly all of their large brains. Maybe cats used more of what they had.

It didn't bear thinking about. And certainly the fact that Marilyn was the one who'd brought up the whole thing didn't bear thinking about. While it was true that Binky, Cosmo, and Sheba had belonged to Stanley's wife as much as cats ever belonged to anyone and were therefore technically not Stanley's cats, he had become quite attached to them. He didn't think he could give them up. Not even for Marilyn.

"You'll win her over, guys. Don't worry about it."

The cats, who never worried about anything as far as Stanley could determine, slept on.

Stanley, however, couldn't sleep at all. He tried. He had taken a warm bath, washed the smoke off his body and out of his hair (admittedly not a difficult job), turned out the light, and lain down in the bed.

But while his body was relaxed, his mind was racing. He couldn't stop thinking about all that had happened during the evening.

The parts involving Marilyn he was able to put out of his mind, for the most part, but everything else swirled around in his brain like ice in a blender, fragmenting into smaller and smaller parts.

There was no use in trying to sleep, and Stanley

had eventually given up, which was why he was sitting in his chair looking at the cats.

Even watching them sleep wasn't as soothing to him as it sometimes was. He felt the need to do something, but he couldn't think what to do. He tried reading, but nothing he picked up caught his interest. Finally he turned to his desk in desperation and located a yellow legal pad and ballpoint pen in the top drawer.

He clicked out the point of the pen and stared at the legal pad for at least five minutes before he began writing. After a few more minutes, he had a list of all the people he'd talked to about Belinda's murder.

It wasn't a long list, but it helped him clarify his thoughts. As he looked at each name, he tried to recall everything he had discussed with that particular person and what he could have said that might have made them want to ruin his car. Or to kick down his springhouse and then lock him in a smokehouse with a blazing fire.

The thought of the smokehouse made Stanley cough. His throat was still raw, as if he'd smoked three packs of cigarettes all at the same time. And his mouth tasted as if he'd licked the ashtray after smoking them, although he'd brushed his teeth three times. He went into the kitchen and got a drink of cold water. That helped a little. Then he rinsed with mouthwash. That helped a little more.

After settling back at his desk, he read over his list again.

Bill and Caroline were first, followed by Hal, Jim Nugent, Lacy Falk, Ellen Winston, Barry Miller, Tommy Bright, and Corey Gainer.

It was the last name that caught Stanley's interest. Where had Corey been when the movie was over? And what kind of car did he drive?

Then it came to him. Corey drove a distinctive car, a bright red Nissan. There weren't that many bright red cars these days, Stanley thought. Most of them were dark, like his own Lexus, or drab. Stanley could remember when cars were all the colors of the rainbow; in fact, sometimes a single car was all the colors of the rainbow. People nowadays talked about the fifties as if that era had been somber and lifeless, though most of the people who talked that way hadn't been alive at the time. And they had certainly never looked at the cars.

The thought didn't help Stanley much. The car he'd seen hadn't been red. It would have stood out even in the darkness if that had been the case. So it probably hadn't been Corey's car.

But maybe that helped. If the car wasn't red, it was one of the usual five or six drab colors that every car seemed to be painted. Black? Dark blue? Gray?

Stanley closed his eyes and tried to think. And after a while it came to him. It wasn't the car itself that he had noticed. It was some little something about it, something that he'd noticed even in the quick glimpse of it that he'd had.

What was it? Something about the door? That was it, all right. The door. A clean spot on the door, though the car itself had been a bit dirty. Dirt always showed up more on dark colors. The car had been dark, with a clean spot on the door.

Big deal, Stanley thought. What did that mean?

He turned to the cats. "All right, guys. Rise and shine. It's quiz time."

Stanley doubted that the cats even heard him. They seemed to have selective hearing. At times they would come alert at the slightest sound, while at other times even a vacuum cleaner running right by their ears couldn't rouse them.

And if they heard him, they chose to ignore him. Not a one of them so much as twitched an ear.

"You guys are a big help."

Stanley turned back to his list. Everyone on it had had an opportunity to poison Belinda. What about motives?

Beside Corey Gainer's name, Stanley wrote *in-*

*heritance*. That was the best of all the motives, Stanley thought, even if the car hadn't belonged to Corey.

He went back to the top of the list. Caroline. As far as he could tell, she had no motive at all. It was silly to think that a lifelong rivalry over cooking abilities had finally reached the point of murder, and Caroline could not have known that Belinda would be the one eating the salsa, even if jealousy were added to the motive mix.

Bill could have known Belinda's location, of course, and he and Caroline could have cooperated in the murder. Stanley didn't believe it for a minute, however. No one would murder because of some old attachment that was slight to begin with. He refused to write anything by either of their names.

Which was probably a mistake, he thought. It's always supposed to be the person you suspect the least. Someone had told him once that the way to pick the killer on any episode of *Murder, She Wrote* was to choose the person with the least possible motive. Either that, or pick the actor who'd been out of work the longest. It was always one or the other.

That wouldn't work here, he decided. This

wasn't like a TV show. There was a real dead person involved.

And she had been involved with Hal Tipton, no matter how much Stanley tried to deny it to himself because he liked Hal and trusted him. Hal had dated her, and they hadn't had an easy relationship.

Stanley reminded himself that he hadn't been back to the barn to see what had happened to the roach poison. Had Hal taken it? Stanley didn't know. He would check in the morning.

He recalled something else. Bill had said that Belinda was argumentative. Hal had agreed.

But Bill had mentioned more than Belinda's temperament. He'd said that Belinda couldn't keep a secret. She told everything she knew. That was something that Stanley hadn't considered before. What if she had known something dangerous? Whom could she have known it about?

Jim Nugent? Stanley thought it might be interesting to check out what had really happened that night when Nugent had ignored the fleeing robber with the sack full of money. He made a note.

What about Lacy Falk? Barry Miller and Tommy Bright? They had been acting strangely, if you asked Stanley. Something was going on there. He was sure of it.

The trouble was that he didn't know exactly *what* was going on. He could try to find out, though. He made himself another note.

He read over what he had written. It was pretty skimpy. Nothing there was going to lead him to Belinda's killer, but he felt that he was at least making a little progress in that direction.

His eyes kept straying back to Corey Gainer's name. Gainer had acted suspiciously at the movie, and then he'd disappeared. That wasn't like him at all. Could it have been that seeing Stanley there with Marilyn had frightened him?

It occurred to Stanley that a man who owned a movie theater would most likely have a ready supply of roach poison around. You wouldn't want menacing, chitinous insects zipping around in the popcorn kicking the freshly popped kernels in the air with their nasty little feet. A thing like that would put the customers off their feed.

Stanley made another note, put his pad aside, and went to bed. This time, he went right to sleep.

# 29

# Illegal Entry

Stanley went for his walk a bit earlier than usual the next morning. The air was heavy and damp, and the grass under his feet was soaked with dew. Stanley knew what was happening. A low-pressure area was pulling moisture in off the Atlantic, setting up the chance of rain.

He was a little surprised but not disappointed. He'd hoped the good weather might last for a while, but he didn't mind the change. And he didn't mind that he hadn't known in advance that the change was going to occur. One of the things he enjoyed about his retirement and about not watching television was that he never heard weather reports. He was just as surprised as anyone—more surprised, maybe—when the weather changed, and it was nice to be surprised.

No more looking at maps of low and high pressure systems, no more worrying about fronts moving through, no more reading the reports from the weather bureau. Now he could just take things as they came. It was a lot more fun that way.

Stanley opened the barn door and located the light switch easily this time, since he'd brought a flashlight. He flipped the switch, and a quick glance at the shelves told him that the can of poisonous powder had been placed right back where it had always been. He walked over, took it in his hand, and shook it. Probably well over half-full, he thought, wondering how much it would take to kill a person.

He looked at the list of ingredients. There was really only one: boric acid, just as he'd suspected. He replaced the can and left the barn.

He visited the smokehouse and shone his light on the broken door. He wished he knew why someone had shut him inside and blocked the door shut. What kind of threat did he pose?

He had no idea, so he walked on down by the creek to look at the partially demolished springhouse. He would have to give Hal a call as soon as it was daylight. Hal could fix the door and the springhouse in no time at all.

Stanley went back toward the inn. The garden was on the way, so he stopped by to admire his handiwork, what he could see of it. As he stood there looking at his corn, he heard something rustling around among the rows.

Stanley pointed the flashlight, hoping that no one was going to jump out of the corn and hit him in the face with a stick of wood.

A pink-eyed rabbit with quivering ears was caught in the yellow beam. It stared back at Stanley, its nose twitching. Stanley laughed, but only for a moment.

"Get out of here, you rascal," he said, taking a step forward. "I can't have you eating my garden. I'll sic my cats on you if you don't watch out."

The rabbit didn't seem frightened at all, not by Stanley and not by the threat of the cats. He was probably already good buddies with the cats, Stanley thought.

"If you eat one leaf of my lettuce, you're a goner," Stanley said, taking another step.

The rabbit looked at him for a second, then calmly turned around and hopped off into the darkness.

"I guess I showed him," Stanley said, knowing as well as he knew anything that the rabbit would be back. Probably with his entire family.

Oh, well. How much could a rabbit eat, anyway?

The sky was beginning to lighten around the edges of the clouds. Stanley went back to the inn.

"Oatmeal?" Stanley said.

"Taste it," Bill suggested. "You'll love it."

"If Caroline made it, I'm sure I will. I love everything she fixes. But oatmeal?"

"Very healthy," Caroline said. "You said you wanted healthy meals."

"I know, but—"

"No buts," Caroline said. "You ask for healthy, that's what you get."

"It's not exactly what we've been having," Stanley said, wondering how his guests would react.

"You said to break them in easy," Bill reminded him.

"Right, but oatmeal?"

"Try it," Bill said, and Stanley did.

It was good. In fact, it was very good, smooth and creamy and sweet with just a taste of . . . something.

"Cinnamon," Caroline said when he asked. "And there's hardly a gram of fat in there. We'll have some fresh fruit, too, and butter if anyone absolutely has to have it."

"Won't need it," Bill predicted, and Stanley knew he was right.

"Everyone's going to D.C. again," Caroline said. "So we won't have lunch."

She didn't look too pleased about the fact that everyone would be eating in restaurants again.

"What about supper?" Stanley asked.

"Fried fish, but mealed, not battered."

"That's the only way to fry fish, sure enough," Stanley said.

"And hush puppies," Caroline said. "Coleslaw, too."

"Fried food isn't exactly healthy," Stanley said.

"It is the way I fix it. Besides, no one will be having any fat at all for breakfast. If they'll just watch their lunch in D.C., they'll be fine."

"Sounds good to me," Stanley said.

"What are you going to be up to today?" Bill asked.

"I think I'll go to town," Stanley said.

"Don't forget the funeral," Bill said. "Two o'clock."

"The old Higgins cemetery," Stanley said. "I remember."

"I wonder if they'll ever find out who did it," Caroline said.

Stanley nodded. "Sure we will."

"We?" Bill said.

Stanley grinned. "They, I mean."

Bill grinned. "After what happened to you last night, you'd better be careful, Stanley. Somebody's got it in for you, and you don't need to be poking your nose in where it doesn't belong."

Stanley had told Bill and Caroline about his little adventure. They were amazed and concerned. They couldn't understand why anyone would want to hurt Stanley.

And they couldn't understand why he hadn't awakened them the previous evening.

"I didn't want to bother you. There was nothing you could do. And if my kicking down that door didn't wake you up, I wasn't sure anything else could."

"One thing about us," Bill said. "We both sleep pretty hard. And of course with Caroline snoring like she does, it would take quite a noise to get through to us."

"I don't snore," Caroline said, fixing Bill with a hard look.

"Right. And ducks don't take to water, either."

"Never you mind about that. I don't snore any more than you do."

"No use to argue. How's your throat, Stanley?"

Stanley swallowed. "Not bad. It's hardly rough at all today."

"Good. Now I'm gonna warn you about one other thing."

"What?"

"That police chief. Are you getting involved with her?"

"I'm not sure."

"You need to be just as careful with her as you do with whoever locked you in that smokehouse."

"I'm being careful."

Bill grinned again. "Yeah. It looks like it."

Stanley didn't know what to say to that. So he left.

Although Corey Gainer was often around the theater during the day, the place looked deserted to Stanley, who went up to the double door leading to the lobby and peered in through the circular glass set in the top half. It was dark inside, and there was no sign of any activity.

Stanley tried the door, just on the off chance that it was open. It wasn't, so Stanley turned to leave. His foot crunched something on the walk, and he looked down to see what it was.

A cricket. There were crickets all around along the walls and doors, most of them dead. Stanley could see the residue of what appeared to be a white powder in a thin line along the walls.

"I knew it," he said, then looked around to see if anyone had caught him talking to himself. No one had.

Stanley wanted more than ever to have a talk with Corey, and he wanted to look around the theater. He remembered the emergency exit door at the rear of the theater, near the furniture store. He headed in that direction.

Overhead the clouds had thickened. The day had grown dark, and a lively breeze was whipping along the street. There was a low barrel-roll of thunder in the distance.

Since the floor of the theater sloped down, the exit door was located below the level of the street. A stairway had led from the sidewalk down to a heavy steel door, which was supposed to be locked on the inside.

And maybe it was. It always had been during Stanley's youth, but plenty of people swore that all you had to do was jiggle the handle just the right way to get a free pass to the movies.

Sure enough, the stairway was still there, just as it had been all those years ago. The steel door was there, too, looking as if it hadn't been painted in forty years. Stanley looked around. No one was watching him, so he went right on down the steps.

When he reached the bottom, Stanley's head

was below the level of the sidewalk. He saw that the concrete floor was littered with faded candy wrappers, old tissues, not a few crickets, and other things that he was sure he didn't want to recognize. He kicked some of them aside and tried the flaking door.

It was locked.

Thunder rolled again, nearer this time, and several drops of rain, as big as dimes, splattered the concrete and crickets at Stanley's feet. He waited until the next rumble, jiggled the door handle just right, pulled up and back, and the door came open.

Well, he thought, what do you think about that? Corey must have left the door open. And he went inside, closing the door behind him as quietly as he could.

# 30

# Rag Mop

The theater was dark, the only illumination coming from the red EXIT sign above the door that Stanley had entered. The air-conditioning was off, and a damp, musty odor mingled with the smell of stale popcorn. Stanley waited until his eyes had adjusted to the darkness and then walked up the slanting aisle past all the empty seats. He wondered how many people had sat in those seats and been entertained by the images on the screen behind him. Thousands, probably.

Stanley pushed through the door that led to the lobby. He had no idea where the storeroom was, but he thought it might be next to Corey's office.

It wasn't. There was a door there, all right, and a room behind the door. The door wasn't even locked, though Stanley thought it should have been when he saw what was inside the room, whose contents would be quite a temptation to a thief with a sweet tooth. The room was full of cardboard boxes packed with candy. Stanley read the names printed on the boxes: Snickers, Milky Way, Milk Duds, Butterfinger, Hershey's. The whole room smelled of chocolate.

Stanley closed the door and looked around the deserted lobby. Dead crickets were scattered here and there on the thin red carpet. They must have slithered, or whatever it was that crickets did, under the door after getting into the poison outside.

On the opposite side of the lobby was a stairway leading to the balcony, which was no longer in use. Stanley thought he could see a door in the wall at the top of the landing. Maybe that was where the storeroom was.

Stanley went up the stairs and tried the door. It wasn't locked, so he pulled it open. He saw a mop bucket, a mop, a push broom, and a large plastic trash can on wheels. He'd found the storeroom, all right.

He found the light switch, turned on the light, and stepped inside. A short shelf was at the end of the room, and Stanley saw a familiar-looking yellow can on it. He moved aside the mop bucket, stepped around the trash can, and stood in front of the shelf.

The yellow can was exactly like the one in Stanley's barn. He didn't have to pick it up to examine it. He knew.

Now he really wanted to have a talk with Corey. And he should probably tell Marilyn what he'd found. She'd want to know about it, even if it didn't prove anything.

He was about to leave when he heard a noise in the theater. Maybe Corey had finally showed up.

While Stanley wanted to talk to Corey, he didn't want to talk to him right at the moment. It would be more than a little embarrassing for Stanley to have to explain what he was doing in the theater, not to mention what he was doing in the storeroom.

He didn't quite know what to do.

He could try to brazen it out, walk right up and say, "Hi, Corey. Fancy meeting you here."

Or he could close the door and stay in the closet until Corey went somewhere else.

He didn't much like the idea of hiding, and he had no idea what he was going to say if Corey came into the storeroom.

It would sound pretty lame to say, "Hey, Corey, I just wondered if I could borrow your mop."

But maybe Corey wouldn't look in the storeroom. Maybe he was just there to work in his office or look at the collection of movie posters that he was rumored to have there.

Stanley decided to stay where he was. He pulled the storeroom door shut. It moved smoothly on the hinges, without the slightest squeak. Stanley turned the button on the knob that locked the door and switched off the light. Maybe Corey wouldn't have a key.

Now that he was as secure as he could make himself, Stanley tried to get comfortable, which wasn't easy considering the size of the room. It was small and cramped with nowhere to sit except on the mop bucket, which was fitted out with a set of hard wooden rollers that didn't look as if they would conform to the shape of anyone's rear end.

Stanley could hear the muffled sound of Corey moving around the lobby. He heard two doors open and shut, and he wondered what Corey could be looking for down there. He should know where everything was.

And then for the first time it occurred to Stanley that Corey might not be the person who was moving around.

Stanley thought about the smokehouse. His throat started to hurt, and he swallowed to get some saliva down it.

A third door slammed.

Probably the entrance to the concession stand, Stanley thought. Maybe Corey, or whoever it was, wanted to have himself some Milk Duds.

The door slammed again.

Okay. No Milk Duds. He hadn't been behind the counter long enough to get them.

For a second or two it got very quiet. Then Stanley heard heavy footsteps coming up the stairs.

Stanley looked around for a weapon, but he didn't see anything except the mop. Well, it was better than nothing, though not much.

Stanley reached out a hand for the mop, trying to be quiet. He had noticed before, however, that the very time that he was trying to be quiet was the time when he was going to make enough noise to wake a hibernating bear. He'd always thought his seeming clumsiness probably had something to do with eye-hand coordination, but whatever the reasons were, the results were always the same. Whenever silence was worth ten dollars a pound, Stanley regularly seemed to bump against a box or kick a can or drop something.

This time, he didn't do any of those things. In fact, the way he looked at it, what happened wasn't really even his fault.

It happened, he was convinced, because there was no light in the room, or at least not enough light for him to see very well at all. What light there was came in around the edges of the door, and it gave only a vague outline to the objects in the room.

Of course if Stanley had been able to see just a little better, he might not have slipped, and if he hadn't slipped, he might not have fallen against the wheeled trash can.

And if he hadn't fallen against the wheeled trash can, he might not have stumbled toward the back of the room, windmilling his arms and trying not to crash to the floor on his face.

He really, really didn't want to land on his face again. His nose was still tender from his smokehouse tumble.

This time he got lucky. He didn't land on his face. He didn't land anywhere. He stayed upright, but just barely, and in doing so he somehow stuck his right foot in the mop bucket.

The mop bucket, like the trash can, was on wheels, and Stanley's left foot slid across the room, pulling half his body inevitably after it. Almost before he knew it, he was practically doing a split. He managed to get a hand on top of the trash can and stop his slide before he pulled himself in two like a wishbone.

Someone was outside the door, rattling the knob.

Stanley let go of the trash can and grabbed the

mop handle. He pulled his legs together, but he couldn't get his foot out of the bucket.

"Come out of there!" a voice demanded.

Come in and get me, Stanley thought but didn't say. He wasn't coming out for anyone. He brandished the mop handle, ready for anything.

Well, almost anything. He wasn't ready at all for what happened next.

The doorknob exploded.

A surge of adrenaline shot through Stanley's body like an electric shock. Stanley's ears rang and he slashed downward with the mop. He didn't hit anything except the door, however.

As if in response to the blow, the door swung inward and slammed against the wall. Stanley backed up as fast as he could, dragging his bucketed foot along, appalled at what he saw.

Officer Mike Kunkel, utility belt and all, stood in the doorway, his legs spread apart, his pistol held firmly in a two-handed grip and pointed straight at Stanley.

Kunkel looked Stanley up and down as if he were examining an exotic species of wild game.

"All right, Waters. Drop that mop and come out of there with your hands up."

When the corn wears a heavy coat,
you'll soon need one of your own.

Take off your coat on a winter's day,
and you'll gladly put it on in May.

# 31

# My Bucket's Got a Foot in It

Stanley felt like a complete idiot. The only good thing about the whole ridiculous situation was that no water was in the bucket.

Well, there was one other thing. There were no cameras around. Thank goodness for small favors.

Kunkel twitched the barrel of the pistol. It looked as big as a sewer pipe to Stanley. He really didn't like guns.

"I said drop the mop, Waters."

Stanley dropped the mop.

"Now come out of there with your hands up."

"Can I take my foot out of this stupid bucket first?"

"You don't do anything until I say so." The pistol barrel twitched again. "Now come out of there."

Kunkel backed across the landing to give Stanley plenty of room, and Stanley clattered forward.

Stanley Waters, criminal mastermind. With a mop bucket on his foot.

When he got to the door, he tripped and had to brace himself on the doorframe to keep from falling. The bucket clanged against the wall.

"Watch it, Waters. Don't make any false moves."

"Define 'false moves,' " Stanley said, wondering if falling counted.

"And don't get smart with me. I'm the one holding the pistol."

Yeah, Stanley thought, but I'm the one with the mop bucket.

"Slow and careful. Keep your hands where I can see 'em."

"Don't worry," Stanley said as he emerged from the storeroom. "It's all I can do to stand up."

"Very funny. Okay, stop right there and turn and face the wall."

"I'm not sure I can turn."

"You'd better make a good try. It's either that or hit the floor."

Stanley turned. He felt silly with his hands in the air and started to lower them.

"Keep 'em up."

Stanley kept 'em up.

"Now lean up against the wall."

"Oh, come on, Kunkel. What is this? You're treating me like some kind of criminal."

"Not just some kind. A burglar. You've been breaking and entering. So lean on that wall."

Stanley didn't move. "I didn't break anything. I just entered."

"That's not what old Mr. Folsom says. He saw you sneak down the stairs and come through the exit door."

Old Mr. Folsom owned the furniture store behind the theater. Stanley hadn't known he was watching.

"He couldn't have seen me come in. Anyway, the door was open. I didn't break it down."

"We'll let the jury decide that. Now lean on that wall."

"No, I'll fall down."

"Too bad."

Stanley heard a quick step behind him. Kunkel slapped Stanley's left palm against the wall, then hooked his left instep over Stanley's and jerked backward.

That technique might have worked just fine with a normal felon, but even in that case it might have proved a failure if the felon had been wearing a wheeled bucket on his foot.

Stanley's right foot shot out, and the bucket caught Kunkel solidly on the ankle.

Kunkel screeched and fell to the floor, dragging Stanley along with him.

Stanley landed on top, with Kunkel spasming beneath him. The pistol was lying several feet away, which made Stanley feel much better. At least he wasn't going to get his head, or some other even more vital portion of his anatomy, blown off. He tried to get up, but the bucket kept slipping, which meant that Stanley kept falling back on top of Kunkel.

Every time that Stanley landed on him, Kunkel made a sound something like "Uhh."

He'd probably had the wind knocked out of him in the first fall, Stanley thought, giving up the idea of standing. Instead, he rolled off Kunkel and over to the wall. He lay there for a few seconds, watching Kunkel twitch.

"Are you going to be all right?" Stanley asked after a while.

"Uhh."

"Good. You had me worried for a minute there."

"Uhh."

Stanley sat up and leaned back against the wall. He drew his right foot up and started trying to work it out of the bucket. It wasn't too difficult now that he could use both hands.

When he had extracted his foot, he tossed the bucket back into the storeroom where it rattled across the floor. Stanley stood up and tested his foot. It seemed to be working fine. He thought about picking up the pistol but decided against it. He didn't want to hold it. So he toed it aside and knelt down by Kunkel.

"Are you feeling any better?"

"You . . . must weigh . . . a ton."

Stanley's feelings were hurt. He didn't weigh anywhere near a ton, and he'd lost a great deal of weight since being at his heaviest some years earlier.

"I don't weigh any more than you do. Do you want to stand up?"

Kunkel raised his head and nodded. Stanley reached out a hand. Kunkel took it, and Stanley stood up, pulling Kunkel after him.

Kunkel took a couple of deep breaths and then picked up his pistol. He pointed it at Stanley.

"Now lean up against the damned wall."

Stanley sighed and leaned up against the damned wall.

# 32

# Weatherman Unbound

If there was one thing more humiliating than being caught with your foot in a bucket, Stanley thought, it was being hauled into the Higgins jail dripping wet from the rain that had started pouring from the thick gray clouds.

And in handcuffs.

Geraldine Calloway was back on duty, and when she saw Stanley, she started laughing uproariously. When she was finally able to catch her breath, she said, "You've really topped yourself this time, Kunkel. I'll bet there won't be any crime in Higgins for the next ten years once you get this hard case behind bars."

"Can it," Kunkel said just as Marilyn came into the room from her office.

"What's going on?" she said, and then she saw Stanley.

For a fraction of a second, he thought she was going to laugh, too. Her eyes widened, and her mouth opened, but she got control of herself. "Stanley, what's going on?"

"I caught him red-handed," Kunkel said. "Breaking and entering at the Palace Theater."

The handcuffs were hurting Stanley's wrists, his clothes were wet, and water was squishing from his shoes.

"I didn't break anything. The door was open. I just went in to look around."

"Are those handcuffs?" Marilyn asked.

Stanley held up his hands. Kunkel had been kind enough to cuff him in front since his body search hadn't turned up any weapons more dangerous than seventy-five cents in change and a nail clipper.

"Take off the cuffs," Marilyn told Kunkel. "And then get back out on patrol."

Kunkel was nonplussed. "What? I caught him red-handed. He was stealing stuff."

"What stuff?"

"Well," Kunkel said, his face twisting with thought, "he had a mop."

Marilyn grinned. "Were you stealing a mop, Stanley?"

"No. I was just going to use it to defend myself. It didn't work very well, though."

"Take off the cuffs," Marilyn said again.

Kunkel did it, but he clearly didn't like it. Stanley rubbed his wrists theatrically.

"You come in my office," Marilyn told him. To Kunkel, she said, "And you go out and try to catch some real crooks."

Kunkel didn't say a word. He was almost as wet as Stanley, and he didn't appear to relish the idea of going back outside.

"Did you hear me?"

"Yes'm." Kunkel turned and left.

"And don't tell anyone about this, anyone at all," Marilyn called after him.

"Yes'm," Kunkel said without turning.

"And don't you laugh anymore, Geraldine," Marilyn told the dispatcher. "We'll be lucky if Mr. Waters doesn't sue us for false arrest."

"Mr. Waters," Geraldine said, struggling to look serious. "Right."

"And while you're not laughing, get Mr. Waters a towel."

"Right," Geraldine said.

Stanley followed Marilyn into her office. The small room had green walls, what he could see of them. Flyers were tacked up everywhere—

wanted posters, they looked like. The desk was covered with papers, and there were even papers on the only chair in the room other than the one behind the desk.

"You have a lot of paperwork?"

"I'm just not very well organized. But I know where everything is."

Stanley looked around doubtfully. "I don't see how you keep up with it all."

"I have a good memory." Marilyn moved the papers out of the chair. "Have a seat and tell me what happened."

Stanley sat in the chair. The vinyl seat felt cold against his wet pants, and his clothes were sticking to him.

Marilyn sat behind the desk. "So why did you break into the theater?"

Stanley explained himself as best he could. In the telling, he realized just how weak his reasons had been.

Marilyn did, too.

"You know, Stanley, you really have to think things through before you take action." She smiled. "Not that I don't like a man of action."

Stanley's head did a rapid warm-up at what he considered an implied compliment. He hoped steam wasn't rising off it.

Geraldine knocked at the door but didn't wait for an invitation to enter. She walked over to Stanley and handed him a thin towel that had probably been white sometime during the Truman administration.

Stanley looked at it doubtfully, and Geraldine said, "It's good enough for the prisoners, so it should be good enough for you. You were practically one of them. Anyway, it's clean."

Stanley thanked her as she left the room and began toweling off. He got his head and face dry, but the towel didn't help his clothes much.

"You can leave in a minute," Marilyn said. "First I have a few things to say."

"Go ahead," Stanley said, feeling that he deserved chastisement.

"Let's take that business about the boric acid first. You can buy it just about anywhere, even right off the shelf at the pharmacy. Whoever killed Belinda didn't have to have access to roach killer."

"Oh."

"And I've already talked to Corey today. Didn't you think I'd check on him?"

"Well . . . I didn't think about that."

"I guess you didn't. Anyway, Corey got sick last night, just like we were told. He had stomach problems, and he went right to bed."

"How do you know?"

"He told me. And I saw him. He's not much better this morning, and if he's faking the pasty color of his face, then he's an acting genius."

"Oh. I was probably a little impetuous, then."

"I'd say that. And you were breaking and entering, weren't you?"

Stanley remembered what an accomplished liar he was becoming. I've started down the slippery slope, he thought. But that didn't stop him from saying, "No, I wasn't. The door was open, and I just went inside."

"Just like we used to do when we were kids. As I'm sure you remember."

"You did that?"

"Just once. And I got caught. What about you?"

"I might have used the door once or twice. I didn't get caught, though."

"You did this time."

Stanley gave her his best contrite look. He thought he did contrite just about as well as anyone. "And I've learned a very important lesson."

"I certainly hope so."

"And you know what?"

"What?" Marilyn asked.

"Nothing that's happened has eliminated Corey as a suspect. He still has the best motive of anyone."

"Maybe, but that doesn't mean he did it."

"I know that."

"And you haven't asked me what else I found out from Corey Gainer. You have to get all the information, Stanley, not just part of it."

Stanley tried the contrite look again.

"Are you sure you're feeling all right? You don't look so good."

Stanley thought that maybe he'd overestimated his ability to look contrite. "I'm fine. What else did you find out?"

"I found out that Barry Miller and Belinda had quite an argument one night after they went to the movies. They'd seen *Key Largo,* and Belinda was arguing that the colorized version she'd seen on TV was better. She even said that she liked the colorized version of *Casablanca.*"

"Barry mentioned that, but he said it was no big deal."

"That's not what Corey said. He said that the two of them got quite loud and that Barry's face turned as red as Tommy Bright's car."

"Why would he lie to me?"

"People lie for lots of reasons. But one reason is to keep you from being suspicious of them."

"So you think Barry killed her?"

"I didn't say that."

Stanley shivered. His wet clothing wasn't getting any drier.

"You don't think he killed her?"

"I don't know," Marilyn said. "Maybe he did. We don't have enough information yet."

"What about whoever hit me over the head?"

"I sent out an investigator this morning. He didn't find anything."

"Great," Stanley said, shivering again.

"You'd better go home. Take a hot bath. Are you going to the funeral?"

"I'll be there."

"Me, too."

# 33

# Funeral in the Rain

The church service was short, though not particularly sweet. The Reverend Mr. Turner hadn't known Belinda well, which helped with the brevity but which didn't do much for the sentimental aspects of the service. Stanley didn't mind. He was keeping his eyes open to see if any of his favorite suspects did anything to reveal their guilt.

They were all there: Barry and Tommy, Lacy Falk, Jim Nugent, and Bill and Caroline, though the last two didn't count since Stanley didn't suspect them. And none of the others did anything in the least suspicious. Everyone in fact looked a bit teary-eyed, and Lacy even had to use her hanky a time or two during the singing of "When We All Get to Heaven," a real tearjerker that Belinda had apparently requested in some document found in her safe-deposit box.

Ellen Winston was sitting with the family, of whom there were only a few members, including Corey Gainer, who was going to inherit all Belinda's money. Stanley still thought Gainer was the best suspect in the murder, though admittedly he looked as sick as he claimed to be, nothing at all like a man who could hit Stanley in the head with a log and then lock him in the smokehouse.

Gainer was as teary-eyed as anyone, too, except for Ellen, who was clearly distraught. She was bent over with weeping, and her shoulders shook as she cried. Corey put his arm around her, but it didn't seem to help.

Stanley was glad that he was sitting several rows behind her. If she still blamed him for Belinda's death, there was no telling what she might do.

When the service was over, Stanley avoided speaking to Ellen and the family and headed directly to his car. He didn't see Marilyn in the parking lot, though she had been standing in the rear of the church during the service. She must already have gone to the cemetery.

The sky was still overcast, the clouds still thick and heavy. It was going to rain again any minute if

Stanley was any judge of weather conditions. And he was, even if he didn't have the United States Weather Service to advise him, and even if he'd left his umbrella in the car. He walked a little faster. He didn't want to get wet again.

The old Higgins cemetery wasn't far from the center of town. For that matter, nothing in Higgins was far from the center of town. Stanley eased his car (the one with the long scratch down the side, he thought) into the funeral procession. As he drove, he considered Belinda's death and wondered again why anyone would want to kill her.

He still couldn't think of a single reason.

An argument about colorized movies? Ridiculous.

A fight about hairstyling? Preposterous.

A dispute about who was going steady with Barry Miller? Laughable.

A nearly forgotten event from the distant past? Absurd.

There had to be more to it than that, but Stanley couldn't for the life of him figure out what it was. He had the feeling that he already had some of the information he needed, that it was bouncing around there in the dark in the back of his head like a loose basketball in an empty gymnasium, but if it was, he couldn't make it stop bouncing and let him look at it.

As he drove through the gates of the cemetery, the sky grew darker and a slow rain began to fall. Water dripped off the pine needles, splatted on the roof of Stanley's car, and blurred his sight of the taillights in front of him. He turned on the wipers, and they swished the water away.

The procession stopped in front of the gravesite. The casket was already there, elevated and surrounded by flowers. A green canopy had been erected beside the grave. Ellen and the family members sat under it, while the Reverend Mr. Turner stood by the casket, not seeming to mind the rain.

Stanley parked his car and got out, raising his umbrella. The rain ticked against it and dripped off the rim. Stanley looked down the narrow cemetery road to the plot where his mother and father were buried. The headstone was a dusky blur in the rain. He told himself that he would come back in a day or so and put some flowers on the graves.

Jim Nugent was parked nearby, wearing a hat but not holding an umbrella. Stanley thought about saying something to him, but Nugent glared at him from under the hat brim, and Stanley changed his mind.

Through the curtain of rain, Stanley saw a police car parked at the end of the procession. Someone got out, and a large black umbrella unfurled. Stanley couldn't tell who was holding it, but he supposed that it was Marilyn. Soon there were umbrellas all around, as if a field of black mushrooms had sprung up in the sudden dampness.

The Reverend Mr. Turner said a few words, read a psalm, and the funeral was over. Stanley knew that it was customary to go over and say sympathetic words to the family, but he didn't think he'd do so. He didn't know them, except for Corey, and he didn't want to face Ellen. She was still crying, and he was afraid that she might get hysterical if she saw him. He would wait a few days and talk to her when she had calmed down.

He was ducking back into his car when he noticed that Jim Nugent was leaving. When Nugent swung open his car door, Stanley noticed the magnetic sign on the side. Something clicked into place in his head.

The car was a little dusty, the dust spattered by the rain, but that wasn't it, at least not entirely. There had been something about the car on the side street near the inn that Stanley had thought about the previous night but that had not registered in his conscious mind during the day. Not until now, that is, when it had jumped right into the forefront.

The basketball had stopped bouncing, and Stanley held it firmly in his hands.

There had been a clean square in the middle of the car's dusty front door, just exactly like the place that might be made if a magnetic sign was pulled off.

Stanley stood up and started toward Nugent, who glanced over his shoulder and saw him. Instead of waiting for him, Nugent jumped into the front seat, started his car, and took off.

Stanley turned and ran back to his own car. Not worrying now about getting wet, he lowered the umbrella and tossed it in, then lunged in after it. There were cars in front of him and behind him, but he did a quick back-and-fill and spun out after Nugent, who already had a pretty good start.

The roads in the cemetery didn't have any long straightaways, however, and Nugent had been forced to maneuver around quite a few twists and turns. He hadn't gotten far, but he beat Stanley to the cemetery entrance, where he accelerated rapidly through the gates and down the street.

Stanley knew that everyone at the funeral would

be wondering what was going on. He looked in his rearview mirror but saw only blurred faces that seemed to be staring blankly in his direction. Then he put his eyes back on the road and put the pedal to the metal.

The Lexus responded gleefully, not bothered at all by the scratch down the side. Stanley was generally a careful driver, and the car seemed glad of the chance to show off.

Nugent might have been a careful driver, too, under normal circumstances. Stanley had no way of knowing. Now, however, Nugent was driving like a maniac, going much too fast for a populated area and much too fast for the rain-slicked streets.

The good thing about the rain, as far as Stanley was concerned, was that it was keeping most people inside. That meant a lot less chance that either he or Nugent was going to run over someone.

Stanley wondered why Nugent had taken off. Probably he realized that Stanley had figured out who his attacker had been. Instead of trying to brazen it out, Nugent had decided to make a run for it.

It was a typical cowardly reaction, Stanley thought. Just the kind of thing you'd expect from a sneak, or from someone who'd resort to poison instead of some more direct method of murder.

Stanley wondered if Nugent's having to leave the police force had been festering in him for thirty years or more. It certainly looked that way. But it wasn't festering any longer. Nugent had taken his revenge, and he'd tried to kill Stanley for getting too close to the truth.

And now it was up to Stanley to catch him.

# 34

# Deadman's Curve

Well, maybe it wasn't entirely up to Stanley. He heard the sound of a police siren behind him, and a quick glance in the mirror showed him the flashing red and blue of the light bar wavering in the rain.

The smart thing would have been to pull over and let Marilyn catch up with Nugent, but Stanley didn't want to do that. He told himself that he didn't want to because he was the only one who knew why he was chasing Nugent in the first place, but that wasn't really the case.

The real reason he didn't want to pull over was that he wanted to be the one to bring the murderer in. Stanley had been on the case from the beginning, he'd figured it all out, and he wanted to get the credit. Sure, maybe it was a little bit egotistical of him to feel that way, but he believed that he had a right to catch the bad guy.

If he lived long enough.

He spun the wheel and snapped the Lexus around another corner and almost lost control of the car, which seemed somehow to lose its footing. It was leaning so far to the right that its left tires weren't touching the ground.

Things like that had always looked exciting to Stanley in the movies, but he wasn't at all excited now, at least not in the same way. He was scared to death.

The wheel whipped in his hands, but he got hold of it, took a tight grip, and leaned as far as he could to the left. For the first time in years, he wished that he'd never gone on such a successful diet.

After an agonizing moment, during which the Lexus slid along on two wheels through the hazy rain, it settled back to the pavement with a thump that Stanley felt all the way up his spine. He resisted the urge to wipe his brow and kept his eyes on Nugent's car, now two blocks ahead of him.

Marilyn was nearer, only a block back and closing. Stanley didn't think she'd be happy when she caught up with him. She might even want to give him a ticket for reckless driving.

He didn't much blame her, but he wasn't stopping.

Nugent ran the red light at one corner of the town square, sped past the City Hall, and ran the light at the next corner, too. Stanley gritted his teeth and did the same, hoping that he'd be as lucky as Nugent had been. He also hoped that lightning wouldn't strike him. He'd never deliberately run a light in his life.

He sailed through the first light with no trouble, not a car in sight in either direction.

He wasn't so lucky at the second. He heard the screeching of brakes and the angry sound of a horn.

Looking to his left, he saw an electric blue pickup swerving from one side of the street to the other as the driver fought to keep it under control with one hand and bore down on the horn with the other.

Stanley shot through the intersection with inches to spare as the pickup slid broadside past his rear bumper. Watching in the rearview, he saw that Marilyn's car managed to miss the pickup, too, but only by swinging halfway up onto the sidewalk and bouncing around like a toy car tossed by an angry child.

She really was going to be annoyed, Stanley thought.

But even as he thought it, a feeling of exhilaration zinged through him. He had broken the law, and it was good. He had run two red lights, and he'd had a narrow escape, but he had lived to tell the tale. Maybe he *was* a hard case, just as Geraldine had said.

Or maybe he was getting a little crazy. He tightened his hands on the wheel and followed Nugent, who was headed out of town toward Alexandria at eighty miles an hour.

In the midst of Stanley's exhilaration, one little thing bothered him, especially at that speed. Not more than a mile down the road was a sharp curve that had been there for as long as anyone could remember, in spite of occasional appeals to the state's highway department to do something about it. It was a tricky place to navigate, even under ideal conditions, and more than one car had gone flying off the road and into the pines beyond.

Stanley remembered a story that he'd heard when he was in high school. Supposedly two boys had tried taking the curve one night at a speed of nearly a hundred miles an hour in a souped-up Mercury. They hadn't been successful. The car had kept going in more or less a straight line and had taken flight when it left the road.

According to the version of the tale Stanley had

heard, the flight of the car had come to a sudden stop when the vehicle met the bole of an ancient pine tree, and both young men had been catapulted through the car's windshield in a shower of glass.

The next morning they had been spotted in the top of another pine, fifty feet high and a hundred yards away. The younger of the two had been impaled on one of the pine's branches and dangled there like a scarecrow.

Stanley felt his palms begin to sweat. Was he going to let himself be scared by some old story that had probably been made up by mothers of teenage sons to scare them into driving sensibly and that most likely didn't have a grain of truth in it?

Or was he a hardcase red-light-runner breaker-and-enterer who feared nothing?

It didn't take him long to decide that he wasn't a hard case after all, not by a long shot. He eased off the accelerator and applied the antilock brakes. The Lexus began to slow.

Stanley hadn't been any too soon. Up ahead Nugent's brake lights flashed on as he entered the curve, but he hadn't thought about the curve as Stanley had. He'd gone in too fast.

Smoke poured from under Nugent's car as the brakes locked.

Old Jim should have gotten the antilocks, Stanley thought as Nugent's car slid straight off the road.

It didn't get to the trees, however. It hit the shallow drainage ditch that ran beside the road, flipped, and rolled over twice.

Stanley had been to the movies; he knew what would happen next—the car would burst into flames and explode in a ball of orange flame. He had to try to get Nugent out before that happened.

He was out of his car and halfway across the ditch when Marilyn called to him.

"Stanley, stop right where you are! I've radioed for help. We'll let the professionals handle this. They're trained for the job. We aren't."

Stanley turned and brushed water out of his eyes. Marilyn, wearing a hooded yellow slicker, was coming toward him through the rain.

"But what if the car explodes?" Stanley said.

"Then Jim will blow up. But there's no reason for you to blow up with him."

That made sense to Stanley. He stopped and waited for Marilyn.

"I don't see any fire," Stanley said.

"It's usually not like that. Except on TV. They always blow up on TV."

"And in the movies."

"And in the movies. Right. But it doesn't happen often in real life. Not unless the wreck causes a gas leak. Then any kind of spark can set it off. When that happens, you get an explosion."

"Do you smell gasoline?"

"No, but that doesn't mean there isn't any. It wouldn't take much to cause an explosion, believe me."

"I think I like explosions better in the movies than I would close up and personal."

Marilyn nodded inside her hood. "Most people do."

Stanley heard sirens in the distance. "The professionals."

"That's right. They'll get Jim out. Why were you chasing him, anyway?"

"Because he killed Belinda."

# 35

# Q&A

"You're crazy," Jim Nugent said. "I never killed anybody in my life."

He was lying in a bed in the Higgins General Hospital, a small facility with only two doctors on staff. The room was small, too, and lit by a bright fluorescent light that gave a strange tint to the bluish white walls and didn't do much for the pallor of Nugent's face, either, for that matter.

Nugent hadn't come out of the wreck without damage. He looked to Stanley a little like a man in an old black-and-white cartoon, with his right arm in a cast and suspended in some kind of rope-and-pulley contraption that was similar to the one that held up his right leg. Nugent wasn't going to be behind the wheel of his car or taking part in any major athletic events for quite some time. Or any minor ones.

And it served him right for driving recklessly, Stanley thought.

"If you didn't kill Belinda, why did you run away from Stanley?" Marilyn asked.

She had allowed Stanley to come into the room with her when she talked to Nugent only because Stanley had begged and wheedled and generally made a pest of himself. His best argument, he thought, was that since he had provoked Nugent's flight, it stood to reason that Nugent was afraid of him.

"I can probably help you get a confession," Stanley had insisted.

Marilyn hadn't appeared convinced, but she'd given in, and that was good enough for Stanley. He had promised to behave himself, and he had quietly stood by while Marilyn read Nugent his rights off a little card. Stanley was going to ask her later why she didn't just have them memorized. That way she wouldn't have to carry the card. But he wasn't going to ask her now. He was being good.

In fact, Stanley hadn't said a single word since entering the room, but because of Marilyn's last question he felt he just had to say something now, even though he knew that doing so would probably annoy Marilyn.

"He ran because he was afraid. He knew that I was onto him. That's why."

Marilyn gave Stanley a disgusted look and he clapped his mouth shut. Not only should he have kept quiet, but he shouldn't be trying to put words in Nugent's mouth. He looked around for a place to hide. There wasn't anywhere, however, except the tiny bathroom and the even tinier closet. He supposed that he could attempt to cram himself behind the unbearably uncomfortable-looking vinyl-covered chair, but he didn't think that was worth a try. So he stood his ground and tried to look confident.

"I wasn't afraid of you," Nugent said, setting his mouth stubbornly. It would have been more effective if his face hadn't been covered with tiny unbandaged cuts. "And I wasn't running. And I never killed anybody."

Stanley forgot the look Marilyn had given him. "But you were at my inn last night. You can't deny that. I saw your car parked nearby. You kicked in my springhouse, and you tried to kill me by locking me in the smokehouse. If you try to deny it, I'll—"

Stanley stopped for a second to think what he'd do, and to see if Marilyn would try to shut him up.

She didn't, so he said, "I'll break your other arm."

"You can't threaten me. Isn't that right, Marilyn? He can't threaten me, can he?"

"That's Chief Tunney to you. And while *I* can't threaten you, Stanley can. He's not an officer of the law."

Stanley grinned like an evil hardcase red-light runner.

"Baloney," Nugent said, apparently unimpressed.

"I wrote your license number down," Stanley said. "I have it right here."

He reached in his shirt pocket and pulled out the slip of paper on which he'd written his notes the night before. It didn't have any license number on it, but Stanley didn't think Nugent could see that from where he was lying in the bed.

"It's right here. Want me to read it off to you?"

Nugent was silent for a few seconds. Then he said, "You could have written that down anytime."

Maybe Stanley couldn't look evil, but he was confident that he was now a pretty good liar. "But I didn't write it down just any old time. I wrote it down last night when I saw your car, and I'll swear to that in court."

This time Nugent was more impressed. "All right, maybe I was at your inn last night, but that doesn't mean I did anything. I was just walking around."

"We have the log you braced against the door," Marilyn said. "It has your fingerprints on it."

Stanley looked at Marilyn with admiration. She was an even better liar than he was, but then she'd had a lot more practice.

Nugent was silent for a bit longer than he'd been after the license-number gambit. Stanley was beginning to think he wasn't going to respond at all.

"I don't think you can get fingerprints from a log," Nugent said at last.

"Things have changed since you were on the force," Marilyn said. "We have better methods and better equipment. We can get prints off nearly anything."

Nugent furrowed his brow. It didn't improve his appearance a bit. "All right. I was there. I kicked the springhouse in." He looked at Stanley balefully. "I'll pay you for it."

"That's not good enough. Money can't make up for the fact that you tried to kill me."

"No, I didn't."

"You locked me in the smokehouse. I could have died from inhaling all that smoke."

"There wasn't much smoke," Nugent protested,

not bothering any longer to deny what he'd done. "I made sure the fire would burn out pretty quickly, so you were never in danger. I just wanted to scare you."

"Well, you didn't. You're the one who was scared because I'd figured out that you were the one who killed Belinda."

Nugent grimaced. "Don't start that again. If you believe I killed anyone, you're crazy."

Stanley looked at Marilyn. "This is where we came in. But we don't have to listen to it again. You know he's guilty. Arrest him."

"You're worse than crazy," Nugent said. "You're crazy and stubborn."

"I always get my man. Arrest him, Chief Tunney."

Marilyn didn't say anything. She just stood there looking at Nugent. Her arms were crossed over her chest, and her right foot was tapping the floor.

"What's going on? Why don't you arrest him?"

"Because she knows I'm telling the truth, dumbass."

Stanley bristled. "There's no call for that kind of language in front of a lady."

"She's no lady. She's a cop."

"That does it," Stanley said, advancing on the bed. "I'm going to break your other arm."

"You're not going to do anything of the kind," Marilyn told him, putting out a hand to stop him.

"Don't worry," Nugent said, raising his head and resting on his left elbow. "I'm not afraid of him. Let him try. I'll bust him one in the eye."

"With what?" Stanley asked. "Your cast?"

Nugent glared. "You big bag of wind."

"You worthless rent-a-cop."

"You washed-up weatherman."

"You sorry excuse—"

Marilyn's sharp voice cut into the less than witty exchange. "*Stanley!* Stop that."

Stanley looked sheepish and felt his head warming up. He knew he'd been acting like an eighth-grader.

"This is all my fault," Marilyn said.

"Huh?" Stanley said. "How could it be your fault?"

"Don't tell him," Nugent said.

"Tell me what?"

"That Jim asked me for a date," Marilyn said.

"He did?"

Nugent sank back into his pillow. "I asked you not to tell him."

"You asked her for a date?"

"I turned him down, Stanley."

"Huh?"

"You might as well give up," Nugent said. "He's so dumb he wouldn't get it if you printed it in pencil on a Big Chief tablet."

Stanley looked from one of them to the other. "Get what?"

"Never mind," Nugent said. "Why don't you just get out of here and leave me alone."

"That might be a good idea," Marilyn said. "Stanley, why don't you go out in the waiting room while I take Mr. Nugent's statement."

"But—"

"Don't talk," Marilyn said. "Just go."

Stanley balked. He wanted to find out what was going on. But he saw from the look on Marilyn's face that she wasn't going to give in.

"I think I'll go outside and wait for you," he said.

"Good. I'll be out in a minute."

"I'll read a magazine or something."

"Fine."

"I'll be right there if you need me."

"I won't need you, Stanley. I can take care of myself."

"I know that. I didn't mean anything."

"Then get out of here." Nugent's eyes were

closed. "I'm tired of listening to you. I'm tired of looking at you, too."

Stanley started to say something, but he couldn't think of anything that didn't sound like an eighth-grader. So he just opened the heavy door and let it swing shut behind him as he went out to the waiting room.

---

Spider webs floating at sunset
mean an evening frost.

When hornets build nests high in the tree, the
winter will be mild and free.

When there are fireflies in great number,
the weather will be good.

---

# 36

# Car Talk

Stanley wasn't impressed with the waiting room. Granted, the chairs weren't vinyl covered, but there were only three of them, and they were small. The magazine selection left something to be desired, as well. Stanley wasn't interested in reading a three-year-old issue of *Motor Trend* or an even older issue of *Family Circle*.

He was thumbing through a raggedy copy of *Cosmopolitan* when Marilyn came up to him.

"Getting any good tips?" she asked.

Stanley closed the magazine and put it back on the shelf. "Not really. Did Nugent confess?"

"We need to talk, Stanley." Marilyn looked over her shoulder at the nurses' station. "But not here."

Stanley stood up. "Fine. Where?"

"How about outside?"

Stanley nodded. "Let's go."

Although the rain had stopped earlier, the outside was even less satisfactory than the waiting room. It was past eight o'clock, and the hospital's outside lights were drawing bugs—crickets and moths.

"Maybe we could sit in the squad car," Marilyn suggested.

"Good idea."

They walked down the long sidewalk that led from the hospital's front door to the parking spaces that lined the curb. Those spaces were reserved for the doctors and the handicapped. The squad car was parked in the lot across the street.

Neither of them said anything until they were inside with the doors shut. It was too warm and humid to leave the windows up, however.

"Why don't you start," Stanley said.

Marilyn nodded. "All right. There's not really much to tell. Jim asked me for a date the other day, and I turned him down. He—"

"Wait a minute. When did he ask you?"

"It was the day after your grand opening. He called me up and we talked for a while. Then he asked me to go to dinner with him."

"That's all?"

"Well, there was a little more to it than that. He

said a few things that were very flattering. I liked hearing them."

Stanley thought he could say flattering things, too, though he probably needed a little practice. A few tips probably wouldn't hurt, either, but he certainly wasn't going to ask Nugent. He wondered if there might be something in the issue of *Cosmo* that he had overlooked.

"What did he say?" he asked.

"Never mind that. It doesn't matter."

She was right. And Stanley wouldn't want to use any of Nugent's lines, anyhow.

"And you turned him down?"

"Yes. He didn't like it at all, in fact, and he decided to take it out on you."

"Why take it out on me?" Stanley asked, though the top of his head was already turning red.

Stanley was glad that it was dark inside the car. Even if the parking lot was fairly well lit, Marilyn wouldn't be able to see his embarrassment.

"Because I told him that I didn't want to go out with him."

"But that doesn't have anything to do with me."

"I know. But when he pressed me for a reason, I told him that I was going out with you."

"Oh . . . But you weren't."

"I know, but I thought it was just a matter of time. And it was, wasn't it?"

"I guess so." Stanley resisted the urge to reach up and feel the top of his head, which he estimated was by now giving off as much heat as the griddle on Caroline Caldwell's stove on pancake day. "You were pretty sure of me, weren't you?"

"I wouldn't say I was sure. I was just hoping."

Stanley found that he was more or less amazed. It wasn't that women didn't find him interesting. They did, but in the past he'd suspected that at least some of their interest had come from the fact that he was a well-known TV personality. And he wasn't interested in them, anyway. He'd always been happily married, and the idea of being unfaithful to his wife had never entered his mind.

Now, however, things had changed. And Stanley wasn't sure of the rules.

Marilyn was, however. She leaned across the seat and kissed him on the mouth.

Stanley was surprised, but not so much that he didn't kiss her back.

"That was nice," Marilyn said after they parted. "But this probably isn't the place for it."

"No, I guess not," Stanley said, not so sure that he agreed. "And you still haven't told me all about Nugent."

"Oh. Do you really want to hear it?"

Stanley really did.

"All right. Jim thought about what I'd told him, and the more he thought about it, the madder he got. Then you paid him a little visit. That didn't help."

"I can see why it wouldn't," Stanley said, remembering that Nugent hadn't been at all pleased with the questions Stanley had asked.

"And then he saw us coming out of the movie. He was in town on a job and just happened to drive past when the feature was over."

I'll bet, Stanley thought. "I didn't see him."

"Well, you weren't looking. Anyway, he's the one who keyed your car."

"That good-for-nothing—"

"Now, Stanley. Don't be angry. He'll pay you for what he did. You have to understand that he was upset. And when he saw us together, he sort of snapped. After he keyed your car, he went out to your place to wait for you."

"What was he planning to do, beat me to a pulp?"

"Maybe. But he didn't. He decided to take it out on your property instead."

Stanley wasn't mollified. "And then he tried to kill me."

"He wasn't trying to kill you. He was just trying to scare you."

"Well, he didn't."

"Yes, he did."

"Okay. Maybe a little. He *could* have killed me. I was lucky to get out of that smokehouse alive."

Marilyn smiled. "I'm glad you did, though. You can file charges against him if you want to."

"I'll think about it. So you don't think he killed Belinda?"

"No. He's a little hot-tempered, and he acted without thinking of the consequences, but he won't do it again."

Stanley wasn't so sure. "He's hot-tempered, and he acted without thinking. Wouldn't you say that's a pretty good description of Belinda's killer?"

"Not at all."

"Okay. If he didn't kill her, why did he run this afternoon at the cemetery?"

"He was afraid you knew what he'd done at the inn. And even if you didn't know, he didn't want to talk about it. He was embarrassed. Not just because of what he'd done, but because he knew that I preferred you to him."

Stanley wondered if it was as hot in the car as it seemed to him, or if he was heating up all over. He rolled the window all the way down on his side of the car.

"Why did you say that whoever killed Belinda wasn't hot-tempered and didn't act without thinking?"

"That's something *I've* been thinking about. I found out earlier today that the poison was definitely in the salsa. It was loaded with it."

"Don't start up about Caroline and Bill again. I just don't believe it."

"Then there's something you have to account for."

"What?"

"How did the poison get in the salsa?"

"Someone put it there."

"When?"

"After it was already on the table. There were several people standing close enough."

Marilyn nodded in agreement. "Fine. Now think about this. The poison had to be in something, right?"

"Sure."

"So what was it in?"

"What do you mean?"

"It wasn't in somebody's hands. It had to be in a container of some kind."

Stanley remembered that Kunkel had roped off the table area to keep people away.

"Did you find anything?" he asked.

"No. So where did the container go?"

"I don't know. Do you?"

"No. But we have to find it to clear your friends."

The car was no longer warm. In fact, Stanley was feeling a quiet chill.

"We'll find it, then," he said.

# 37

# Dawn

The next day was drizzly and dreary. A gauzy mist hung in the air, and the sky was so heavy that it seemed to sag all the way to the tops of the pines down by the stream, which had been muddied by the rainfall. Water dripped out of the pines and onto Stanley's BLUE SKIES cap.

Stanley kicked a rock. It splashed into the stream, and Stanley squished away through the wet grass up to the goldfish pond. He'd brought a few pellets of fish food, which he tossed in the water. The fish floated up to the top and inhaled the food with hardly a ripple.

Usually Stanley liked watching the fish, but today he didn't take any pleasure in them. He was too busy worrying about who had killed Belinda. It had all seemed clear to him when Nugent had made a run for it, but now he was right back where he had started.

He walked over to the garden, looking for the rabbit, who was nowhere to be seen. He's probably sneaking around at night and eating everything he can find, Stanley thought, but he couldn't detect any damage in the cursory inspection that he made of the tomatoes.

He looked around for the cats. Not a one was in sight. They weren't fond of wet weather, and they were probably all waiting inside for him to feed them.

He didn't much want to go inside. Bill and Caroline were in the kitchen, and Stanley didn't want to talk to them. He knew he wasn't being logical, but he was still convinced of their innocence. Or he thought he was. Could he have begun doubting them?

No. He couldn't. It was just that he didn't have any good explanation for how the poison had gotten into the salsa, not unless one of them had put it there.

He went inside the inn, fed the cats, who twined around his ankles as he poured the food into their bowls, and then went into the kitchen.

It smelled wonderful.

"Waffles," Bill said.

He was sitting at the table with a plate in front of him. Two waffles were on it, both covered in maple syrup.

"Whole-wheat," Caroline said. "Very healthy."

"And I'm sure that syrup is low in calories," Stanley said, his mouth watering.

Caroline shrugged. "I wouldn't say that, but it's fat free."

Stanley sat down. "That's good enough for me. I'll take two."

"Have to put a lot of syrup on them," Bill said. "Else they'll float up off the plate."

"What about butter?" Stanley asked.

"Up to you. Butter's got fat in it, though, and plenty of it."

Stanley decided to take the risk, and when Caroline put the waffles on his plate, he lifted up the top one with his fork and put a pat of butter under it. He lowered the top waffle to let the butter melt.

"That's not much butter," Bill said. "You'll probably be all right."

"I sure will," Stanley said, cutting off a bite and forking it into his mouth, where it practically melted on its own.

"Mmmmmmm," Stanley said.

"Yeah," Bill agreed, looking fondly at his wife. "Best cook in the county. In the state, if you ask me."

Stanley silently agreed. There was no way someone who could cook like that would ever mess up her salsa by putting poison in it.

"That's enough of your bragging," Caroline said to her husband. "You'd better clean up your plate. The guests will be down shortly."

Bill got up, put his plate in the sink, and began washing it. Stanley busied himself with his waffles.

When he was almost done, he said, "Bill, let me ask you something about Belinda. You say that she couldn't get along with people, and that she couldn't keep a secret. Did she know anything really damaging about anyone, something that she might have spread around town?"

"Not that I know about, unless you count Jim Nugent. I still haven't figured out why he didn't go after the robber that time."

"Couldn't be bothered, that's why," Caroline said. "He always was a little lazy."

Stanley wanted to know about his next-best suspects, Lacy Falk and Barry Miller, both of whom had acted suspiciously when he'd talked to them about Belinda. He asked about them.

Bill grinned. "I guess everybody in town knows about that haircut Lacy gave Belinda. But that's about it."

"Nothing about Barry?"

"He and Belinda had a little spat at the Palace one time," Bill said. "Nothing much, the way I heard it."

Stanley had forgotten about that. Barry had lied about his relationship with Belinda, and Tommy Bright had backed him up. Stanley pushed his chair away from the table.

"I'm going to work on the accounts for a while," he said, "and then I'll be going downtown. Give everyone a good breakfast."

Caroline sniffed. "As if they'd get any other kind."

Stanley was headed out when Bill said, "Did they ever find out what kind of poison it was that killed Belinda?"

Stanley remembered that Marilyn had asked him not to tell about the boric acid. It probably didn't make any difference now, especially since it had been established that the poison was definitely in the salsa. Still, Stanley didn't want to betray Marilyn's trust.

"No," he said, "I don't think they have."

Ten minutes later, while he was looking over the grocery receipts for the week, he realized that he knew who had killed Belinda.

# 38

# The Unusual Suspects

Stanley drove downtown. He'd decided not to call Marilyn because there was always the chance that he was wrong. And he didn't think the killer was dangerous. Not anymore.

He parked in the church lot. When he got out of his car, he looked at the long scratch down the side. He was going to file charges against Nugent later if Nugent didn't make good on his offer to pay for the damage he'd done. The scratch ruined the whole appearance of the car.

He left the lot and walked past Bushwhackers. The mist still hung in the air. He looked in the rain-spotted shop window as he passed and waved to Lacy, who frowned and then waved back. In the middle of the block he crossed over the street and went into M & B Antiques.

Barry Miller was inside, dusting off a bicycle.

When he saw Stanley, he stuck the rag he'd been using in his back pocket. He posed by the bike and said, "Ever own one of these when you were a kid?"

Stanley admired the bike. It was a sparkling red and white Columbia, looking freshly waxed, with a spring fork in front and a horn button in the side tanks.

"Never," he said. "I had a secondhand J. C. Higgins. The basic model. My parents couldn't afford anything like that."

"Mine either. But it's a beauty, isn't it?"

Stanley agreed that it was.

"You could probably afford it now. I'd make you a good price."

"I'm sure you would. But I didn't come here to buy a bicycle."

"I'm sorry to hear it. I would make you a real deal."

Stanley shook his head.

"Well, you can't say that I didn't try. What can I do for you, then?"

"You can tell me why you lied about Belinda."

Barry was momentarily taken aback. He raised a hand and smoothed back the wing of silver hair on the right side of his head. "I don't know what you mean."

"About the colorizing. You told me that she liked the colorized version of *Casablanca* but that her attitude didn't bother you. That wasn't true at all. You had quite an argument with her in the lobby of the theater about it. Two people have commented on it, so it was obviously more than a minor disagreement. I'm sure you must remember it."

"I don't, though."

"Yes, you do, Barry. There's no use in lying about it again."

"About what?" Tommy Bright asked at Stanley's back. Stanley hadn't even heard him come in.

"About that stupid colorized movie," Barry said.

"Oh. That."

Stanley turned to look at Tommy. "Yes, that."

"You did lie, Barry," Tommy said. "You might as well admit it."

"You backed him up," Stanley reminded him.

"What are friends for, after all?" Tommy asked.

"I'm not sure lying's part of it," Stanley said.

Tommy shrugged. "Maybe not. But it seemed like a good idea at the time."

"Lots of things do. Tell me about it."

Barry looked angrily at Tommy, who said, "Oh, come on, Barry. What harm could it do?"

"None," Stanley said. "I don't think you killed her, Barry. I just want to know why you lied."

"I don't think that's any of your business."

"Dear me," Tommy said. "Aren't we being noble this morning."

"While he's being noble, fill me in," Stanley said.

Tommy seemed eager to talk. "Certainly. Barry had some strange idea that possibly, just barely possibly, mind you, that Lacy Falk might have killed Belinda."

"Hush, Tommy," Barry said.

"I will not. This is all just too silly." Tommy put a hand on Stanley's arm. "Barry knew that Lacy and Belinda had been fighting, and he thought that some of the fighting was his fault. He's such a handsome brute that he was sure they were fighting over him. So when Belinda was killed, he naturally believed that Lacy was so crazy about him that she'd murdered to have him all to herself." Tommy looked at Barry. "I *told* you it was a ridiculous idea."

"So that's it? You were lying to draw suspicion to yourself to protect Lacy?" Stanley said.

Barry just glared at him.

"That's it exactly," Tommy said, and glanced at his partner. "I'm only telling him for your own good, Barry."

"And I appreciate it," Stanley said. "If it's the truth."

Barry grimaced and gave in. "Oh, it's the truth all right. I know it sounds stupid. It probably *is* stupid. But I thought you were being a little too nosy, and everyone knows that you and the police chief are just like this." He crossed his fingers, and Stanley tried not to blush. "I didn't want you thinking that Lacy had any reason to be angry with Belinda."

Stanley thought about it for a second or two. It made sense, of a kind. After all, it hadn't been twenty-four hours since he'd been acting like an eighth-grader because of a woman, himself. Maybe it was a guy thing.

"That's all I wanted to know," he said. "It was just something I had to check."

He turned to leave, but Barry called him back.

"No hard feelings. Are you sure I couldn't interest you in buying a bike?"

"Not today. I have to go see a woman about a haircut."

Stanley didn't really want a haircut. He wanted to talk to Lacy Falk about some of her own lies. Bushwhackers wasn't particularly busy, so Lacy said that she would talk to him in her office, which was really just a cubicle in the back of the big room, not far from the big hair dryers.

The walls of the cubicle were covered with pictures and calendars of products that Stanley wasn't familiar with. A woman holding a bottle of mane shampoo, for example. Wouldn't that be something that you'd more likely see an ad for in a veterinarian's office? He started to ask about it, but he changed his mind and got right to the point.

"You lied to me about Belinda. The two of you weren't like sisters. In fact, you weren't friends at all."

Lacy sat in the straight-backed wooden chair at her cheap desk, opened a drawer, and brought out something that looked like an elongated leather coin purse that opened with gold snaps.

It wasn't a coin purse, however. She snapped it open and Stanley saw that it held a soft pack of cigarettes. Lacy shook one out and rummaged in the drawer until she found a lighter. She lit the cigarette, taking a deep drag. Then she blew out a long white plume of smoke in Stanley's direction. He could smell it even with the odors of waving lotion and hairspray that filled the place, and he waved his hand in front of his face.

"You mind if I smoke, honey?"

Stanley stifled a cough. He didn't think hard cases would let a little smoke bother them.

"Not at all," he lied. "It's your shop."

Lacy took another puff, let the smoke roll out, and said, "What does it matter to you how Belinda and I felt about each other, anyway?"

"I'm trying to find out who killed her, that's what."

"Well, I didn't."

The top of the desk was covered with papers and she rattled through them until she found a blue glass ashtray. She thumped the Winston on the edge of it and a bit of gray ash fell off the tip.

"I know that."

"Then why in hell are you bothering me, honey?"

"Because you lied, and I want to know why."

Lacy considered the glowing end of the cigarette for a moment, then looked up at Stanley.

"If I tell you, who are *you* going to tell?"

"No one."

"I wish I could believe that."

Stanley looked offended. "I don't repeat things told to me in confidence."

Lacy sighed. "Hell, honey, that's easy to say, whether you mean it or not."

Stanley had to admit that she had a point. "I

mean it, Lacy. It's just something I'd like to know to satisfy my own curiosity."

Lacy took one more drag on the Winston, then crushed it in the ashtray, not even half-smoked.

"All right, then. I lied because I didn't want you to think that Belinda was having any trouble with me or Barry Miller. I guess you know she'd dated him a time or two."

"And you didn't like that, did you?"

"Not a whole lot, honey. But that doesn't mean I killed her. And neither did Barry."

"Are you sure about that?"

"Pretty damn sure. I asked him at the funeral. He said he thought maybe *I'd* done it. You'd think he'd know me better than that. I might strip the dye off a woman's hair, but I wouldn't kill her."

"I didn't think you would."

# 39

# Up on the Roof

The lobby of the General Lee Hotel looked a lot like the outside—faded but respectable. The maroon carpet was badly worn in places, the color all but gone, but it was clean. The huge portrait of General Lee behind the registration desk was faded, too, but the general was still a fine figure of a man.

Walt Mervin was behind the desk. Stanley knew that he was only about twenty-eight or -nine, but he looked twenty years older. The advantage in that was that he had one of those smooth, ruddy faces that would make him look as if he never aged. He might look middle-aged now, but he would also look middle-aged when he was seventy.

Stanley walked over and said good morning.

"Not so good," Mervin said. "It's raining. Keeping all the customers away. Not that we have that many to begin with."

He looked at his visitor as if Stanley might have something to do with the fact that the residency rates at the General Lee were something less than spectacular. Stanley recalled that Ellen had looked at him the same way when she'd heard of his plans to open the inn.

"Where's Miss Winston?"

Mervin looked worried. "I think she's up in the attic. To tell you the truth, Mr. Waters, she's been spending a lot of time up there lately. She really took it hard when Belinda—Miss Grimsby, I mean—died."

Stanley thought that he knew why, but he didn't confide in Mervin. "Do you think she'd mind if I went up and had a word with her?"

"I don't know. But I wish you would. I think she needs somebody to talk to, to tell you the truth. I've tried, but all she does is cry."

"How do I get to the attic?"

"Just take the elevator up to the third floor. Then you can take the stairs to the attic."

Stanley thanked Walt and headed for the elevator.

"It's pretty dusty up there," Mervin called after

him. "I don't know why she goes up there. I really don't."

"Me neither," Stanley said, though he thought he did.

Whoever cleaned the hotel paid little attention to the attic stairs. There was dirt in the corners of the steps, and the tinfoil from a stick of gum glinted in the light from the dusty bulb, from which a wispy strand of spiderweb dangled.

Stanley pushed open the door to the attic without knocking.

"Ellen?" he said, but there was no answer.

No one was in the attic, either. The light was on, and Stanley could see three stacks of dusty cardboard boxes, a set of old box springs, some mildewed mattresses, and several pieces of old furniture: a coffee table, some end tables, and a couple of chairs covered with sheets.

In the middle of the attic, a stair had been pulled down from the ceiling. Stanley assumed that it led to the roof, since he could feel an occasional puff of chilly, damp air. He walked over to the stair and looked up at the heavy gray sky.

"Are you up there, Ellen?" he called.

No answer. Stanley sighed and started climbing the stairs. They seemed to sag forward a little under his weight, but he went on until his head was sticking out above the level of the flat roof, which was covered with a combination of tar and pea-sized gravel. A low wall surrounded the roof on all sides.

Ellen was standing with her back to the north wall, looking at Stanley. She had obviously been on the roof for a while. Her hair was wet and hanging around her face, which was streaked with rain or tears, and her clothes were stained by the dampness.

"What are you doing here?" she said as Stanley climbed out onto the roof with her. Her voice quavered and almost broke, but she didn't cry.

"I just came by for a visit," Stanley said, smiling and trying for a light touch.

It didn't work.

"You came by because you know it's all your fault. You killed Belinda, you son of a bitch."

The language didn't shock Stanley, but what happened next did. Ellen slid down beside the wall and began crying violently, her whole body shaking as the sobs racked her.

Stanley knew that he should not have been shocked. Ellen's grief had always seemed out of proportion to the circumstances, but even now that he suspected the reason, he hadn't thought she would give in to it so fiercely.

He crunched across the wet gravel in Ellen's direction, thinking that he might be able to comfort her, but when Ellen looked up and saw him, it was evident that comfort wasn't what she wanted.

What she wanted was revenge for the death of her friend, the death she still blamed on Stanley. She got to her feet more quickly than Stanley would have thought her capable of doing and rushed him, her hands outstretched, her fingernails aimed at his eyes.

Stanley put up his hands to grab her wrists, but she was too quick for him. Her slight weight was enough to stagger him with the force of her motion and her fury behind it, and she got her hands inside his own, raking her nails down his cheeks, which stung with sudden pain as the skin peeled away in strips.

"You bastard," she panted. "You son of a bitch."

Stanley wanted to tell her that he hadn't done anything, that she'd done it herself, but she wasn't exactly what anyone would define as rational. So he didn't waste his breath.

Instead, he tried to protect himself as she pelted him with blows from her fists. He wasn't able even to slow her down. She drove him steadily away from her, and he realized that he was backing rather too quickly toward the north side of the roof, the side that overlooked the street.

The wall was no more than a foot and a half high.

The street was three stories down, four if you counted the attic.

Stanley was sure that, under the circumstances, the attic should definitely be counted.

He tried to stop, but Ellen kept pummeling him, and he kept right on going back. Much sooner than he would have thought likely, the backs of his knees bumped the wall.

"Ellen," he said, trying not to sound desperate but not doing a very good job of it, "Ellen, stop it or I'll have to hit you."

To his amazement, she did stop. She looked at him, her hair stringing in front of her wild eyes.

"Hit me, you son of a bitch. Kill me like you killed Belinda."

Then she ducked her head and shoved into him with all her might, trying to push him over the wall.

# 40

# Humpty-Dumpty

Stanley dug his heels into the roof about a second too late and found himself dangerously overbalanced, his head and shoulders already out over the wall.

He felt his heels begin to slip on the gravel as Ellen clawed her way up his body as if intent on going over the side with him.

She probably *did* want to go over the side with him, Stanley thought. He resisted the urge to turn his head and look down. He didn't want to know what the street looked like from four stories up, not right now. He wasn't in the mood to have a great fall, and he was pretty sure that he'd be just as hard to reassemble as Humpty-Dumpty.

He gathered his strength and forced himself up and forward, trying to ignore that Ellen was pounding her fists into his bleeding face.

When he was relatively upright, he planted his feet as firmly as he could and braced his calves against the wall, tucking his arms tightly against his chest. Then he thrust his arms outward with all the force he could muster, breaking Ellen's hold on him.

Ellen flew backward a few feet before landing on her backside and sliding across the gravel. Stanley didn't give her a chance to get up. He sprang forward and grabbed both her arms, then knelt astride her with his knees on her shoulders.

She kicked, thrashed, twisted, and arched beneath him, screaming all the while, but she wasn't able to break free, and Stanley was glad of his weight advantage.

Finally she stopped moving, but she kept on screaming, a steady stream of fairly inventive invective that Stanley wouldn't have thought her capable of, even knowing that she was a murderer.

He didn't believe that she had killed anyone intentionally, however.

"Ellen," he said, trying to keep his voice steady. "Listen, Ellen, I know it was an accident. I know you didn't mean to kill Belinda."

Instead of calming Ellen, Stanley's words had the opposite effect. She arched her back with the power of a steel spring, almost tossing Stanley aside. But he kept his grip on her arms and was able to get his knees back in place before she twisted away.

Stanley had never hit anyone in anger. In fact, he hadn't hit anyone at all since the casual fights of his grade school days.

He really wanted to hit Ellen, though. Not because he was angry but because he wanted her to be quiet and to stop writhing around.

But he didn't know how to hit her. He knew that hitting someone could have serious consequences. It wasn't like in the movies where two people could beat each other to a pulp, then get up and smile and walk away as if nothing had happened, and Stanley was afraid that if he hit Ellen too hard, he might do far more damage than he intended.

So he tried talking again.

"Ellen, listen to me. Please. I know what happened, and I know it wasn't your fault. You have to stop trying to hurt yourself and other people and tell Chief Tunney about it. No one's going to blame you."

That probably wasn't true. Plenty of people were going to blame her, but Stanley didn't care. He was past worrying about his lying.

But his lying didn't matter. Ellen didn't even seem to hear him. She spit at him, twisted quickly to the left, and somehow drove a knee into his crotch.

"Urrk," Stanley said, letting go of Ellen and rolling over on his back.

Ellen stood over him and screamed, "I didn't kill anyone! It's all your fault!"

She kicked him in the side, twice, then turned to run. When Stanley saw where she was headed, he struggled to his feet and limped after her.

She got to the wall two steps before he did and put her right foot atop it.

Stanley leaped forward just as she jumped.

# 41

# A New Day

It was a beautiful morning in Higgins. Although Stanley had been up for nearly two hours, reading and walking around the inn's grounds, and although he'd already had a healthy breakfast of hot bran muffins (no butter) and fruit, it was still only a little past sunrise when he drove into the cemetery.

He drove past Belinda's grave, with the fresh earth heaped on top, to where his parents lay under the pines. The sun was shining through the branches and making shifting patterns of light on the graves.

Where the sun never shines, Stanley thought, except that's not true. The sun does shine in the pines, at least some of the time.

He got out of the car and opened the back door. Two pots of chrysanthemums sat on the floor, and he took both of them out to place in front of the low gray granite headstone.

Carved into one side of the stone were his father's name and the dates of his birth and death:

CARLTON WAYNE WATERS
*1919–1990*

On the opposite side was Stanley's mother:

VIRGINIA ANN WATERS
*1921–1991*

She hadn't lived long after her husband's death of a massive heart attack that he had told everyone was nothing more than a slight case of indigestion. Stanley remembered getting the phone call in New York.

As Stanley was arranging the flowerpots, a police car drove up and Marilyn got out. She walked over to Stanley but didn't say anything until he had fixed the flowers to his satisfaction.

"Bill told me I'd find you here. You miss them a lot, don't you?"

Stanley looked down at the yellow mums. "Yes. I just wish there had been something more I could have done for them."

"You made them very happy, Stanley. Your mother talked about you all the time. They never missed *Hello, World!*"

"Speaking of the show, did you happen to watch yesterday?"

"Of course. Didn't you?"

"No TV. I just heard about it."

"That's right. I forgot you don't have a set. You really should get one. They made you look like quite a hero."

"I wasn't much of a hero. If that shirt of Ellen's had ripped, she'd have splattered all over the street."

"I still don't know what kept the both of you from going over."

"The wall. I was able to brace myself and hang on to Ellen with both hands. It's just a good thing Kunkel saw us when he did."

Kunkel had been on patrol, and he'd happened to look up while stopped at the light on the square. He'd rushed to the top of the hotel, along with Mervin, whom he'd picked up in the lobby. With their help Stanley had dragged Ellen back up on the roof. She hadn't been a large woman, but Stanley's arms were still sore. And he thought they might be as much as half an inch longer.

"I'm not so sure Kunkel's glad he saw you. I really don't think he likes you very much, Stanley."

"Gee, that's too bad."

Marilyn hit him playfully in the shoulder. "Your face looks better today."

"Sure it does. I look like I was mauled by one of my cats instead of a Bengal tiger."

"It's not that bad."

Stanley put his fingers up to touch the scratches, but Marilyn took his hand before he reached them.

"I'm still a little upset with you myself, you know," she said.

"Why?"

"You should have come by for me or one of the officers before you went to talk to Ellen. You should always have backup."

"I didn't think she was dangerous. She didn't know how potent the boric acid was. She just wanted a few people to get sick and cause trouble for the inn. She didn't think anyone would die."

"I should have known it was her."

Marilyn was still holding Stanley's hand, but he didn't try to take it away from her. He wasn't wearing a cap, and he wondered if the sun was making his head warm or if the heat was rising because of his contact with Marilyn.

"How could you have known?" he asked.

"It's natural to be upset when a friend dies, but not as upset as Ellen was. That should have made me suspicious. Her grief went way beyond the norm."

"I thought so, too, especially considering the way she acted at Jamar's. But it was what she said to me that afternoon that really gave her away."

"What was that?"

"She said that I'd killed Belinda like a roach, which made me think of the poison. No one was supposed to know about that. And when I remembered that, I thought of something else. We'd both wondered about where the poison was hidden. Ellen was carrying a purse that day. I'm sure that's where it was. She put it there and just waited for an opportunity to use it."

"We should have searched everyone at the scene."

"People got away from there too fast. You couldn't have searched them all, anyway."

Marilyn thought about it, then said, "Maybe not."

"Do you think she'll ever stand trial?"

"Oh, sure. She'll be fine after a few days under a doctor's care, I think. I'm not sure she'll be convicted, though."

Stanley wasn't sure, either. Ellen's intentions had been bad, but she'd never intended murder.

"The funny thing is," he said, "the inn was never a threat to her business. I have only a few guests at a time, and they're people who wouldn't stay in a hotel in the first place. They're just staying at the inn because I was on TV. Otherwise, they'd probably go to Vermont or somewhere."

"Ellen's business hasn't been good for a long time. I guess she didn't see it your way."

"I guess not." Stanley looked down at the headstone again. "Are you about ready to go?"

Marilyn squeezed his hand and sent the temperature of his head up another ten degrees.

"All right. What are you planning next for the inn?"

Stanley smiled. "I got a call yesterday from someone who wanted to know if I'd like to have one of those Civil War battle reenactments there. What do you think?"

"Won't that be expensive?"

"Oh, no. They'll take care of all the expenses. All I have to do is provide a place for them. I think they're hoping to get some TV exposure."

"I wonder what could have given them that idea."

"It's not my fault if they think I might get them

on television. Besides, I've had a couple of calls from *Hello, World!* Now that I'm a hotshot detective, they want to come back and do an interview. They might find the idea of a Civil War battle interesting."

"You have no shame, Stanley. Did you know that?"

"Hey, I didn't make any promises to anyone."

"I'm sure you didn't. Well, I hope nothing goes wrong this time."

"Me, too," Stanley said, thinking of his badly scratched face. "I didn't know this detective business could be so rough."

"It's not always like that. You'll see."

"I will?"

Marilyn gave his hand another squeeze, and his head glowed.

"You never can tell," she said.

The more rain, the more rest.
Fair weather's not always the best.

# 1

# Men in Gray

"I think the uniform makes you look gallant," Marilyn Tunney said.

Marilyn was the Chief of Police of Higgins, Virginia, and Stanley Waters thought she looked a lot better in her uniform than he did in his. She didn't wear hers often, however. She was more likely to be dressed in a Donna Karan suit, as she was today, than her official outfit.

As for outfits, Stanley wasn't exactly sure what a retired weatherman, who now owned a bed-and-breakfast, was doing dressed like a Confederate soldier, anyway.

"You'll really get a lot of publicity for this stunt," Marilyn said, and Stanley suddenly remembered why he was dressed the way he was.

The battle reenactment hadn't been his idea, but

when Barry Miller had suggested it, Stanley had seen the possibilities immediately. Barry was part-owner of M & B Antiques and a passionate reenactor.

Or maybe that was a redundancy. In his brief acquaintance with reenactors, Stanley had yet to meet one who didn't have a passionate interest in what he was doing.

"It gives us a chance to travel in time," Barry had told him. "We don't just put on uniforms and run around out there. We actually *become* people from another era. You should try it, Stanley."

Barry was so enthusiastic about reenactments that he was even growing an unflattering beard that spoiled his matinee-idol good looks and made him look at least ten years older.

At the time, Stanley had not had any intention of trying a reenactment of any sort. His change of mind had come later, after he had talked to Len Wilson, producer of *Hello, World!*, Stanley's old TV show.

Stanley was constitutionally unable to resist the idea of getting publicity for his inn, and while a Civil War reenactment on the grounds would be good, getting it onto network television would be even better.

Wilson liked the idea, too. "But not unless you're involved, Stanley. People still love to see you.

That's why we invite you back to do a forecast every so often. And just think how much your fans would enjoy seeing you as a Confederate soldier."

So there Stanley stood, sweaty and gallant in his wool pants and jacket. He had on a muslin shirt under the jacket, but he couldn't see that it was helping much. He had to keep telling himself not to scratch.

His haversack, slung over his right shoulder, was full of period items: coffee beans, hardtack, a Bible, and eating utensils. He had a cartridge box over his left shoulder, but that was empty, mainly because he didn't have a rifle.

Barry Miller had even tried to persuade him to order a musket from the Dixie Gun Works catalog.

"You can get a reproduction of a three-band Enfield for around five hundred dollars," Barry had said. "That's a rifled musket with flip-up sights and brass fittings. Fires a .577 minié ball and looks great."

But Stanley didn't want a rifle. "I don't think I'm going to make a very good soldier," he told Marilyn.

Marilyn disagreed. "Of course you are." She looked him over critically. "I especially like the hat."

Stanley removed the civilian-style hat, held it in front of him, and looked at it doubtfully. The hat was smashed and wrinkled and dirty, as if several thousand troops had marched across it with muddy boots.

"They told me it was supposed to look this way," Stanley said. "I think the soldiers sat on their hats to keep their rear ends dry, or something like that."

He put the hat back on, telling himself that he wasn't doing so because he was overly conscious of his bald head. Marilyn liked bald guys. Or so she'd said.

"Gallant, huh?" he asked.

"And stout-hearted, too."

He was glad she hadn't stopped with just *stout*. He'd lost a lot of weight, but he still wasn't exactly what anyone would call svelte. He'd been svelte once, he thought, but that had been when he was around thirteen years old and had grown something like six inches taller in one year. Since then, *stout* was probably a much more accurate description.

"Of course you might look a little more authentic in another setting," Marilyn said.

They were standing in the parlor of Blue Skies, Stanley's inn. The parlor was decorated in the style of an earlier day, with most of the furnishings, including the big Philco radio, dating back to the 1930s.

"There were still some Confederate veterans around in the 1930s," Stanley said. "I don't think the last one died until 1959 or so."

"Maybe, but I just don't think the uniform goes with the radio, and the Battle of Higgins wasn't fought in a parlor. Why don't we go outside and have a look at you?"

Stanley wasn't sure he wanted to go outside, but Marilyn insisted.

"Let's go down to the creek," Marilyn said. "When we get back in the pines, we can almost forget it's the twentieth century."

Stanley liked the idea of going back into the pines with Marilyn. They had grown up together, even dated when they were much younger, but they had seldom seen one another since their long-ago graduation from Higgins High. Each of them had married, and their careers had led them in very different directions.

Stanley had gone into radio and later into television, where as the weatherman on *Hello, World!* he had eventually become as well-known as any public figure in America. His face was instantly recognizable to people from Maine to Alaska, from California to Florida. But after the death of his wife, he'd lost his taste for performing on a regular basis and moved back to his hometown, where Marilyn had gone into local law enforcement.

The murder of a guest at the opening festivities of Stanley's inn had brought them together again, and they had been seeing one another fairly often since then. Stanley had even helped solve the murder, and in the process had gained a taste for investigation. However, crime wasn't exactly rampant in small Virginia towns, even if they weren't all that far from Washington, D. C., so Stanley hadn't had any further opportunities to practice his sleuthing skills.

He and Marilyn went out the front door of the inn, Stanley's authentic brogans clomping on the wooden boards of the porch. They left the porch and walked around back, past Stanley's garden, where Stanley had recently done his fall planting. He was sure that the rabbit that had plagued him in the spring was waiting eagerly for the fall crop.

Stanley followed Marilyn down to the creek and into the cool shadows of the trees. There were pines and cedars and plenty of dogwood trees, though the dogwood wasn't blooming now. In the deep shadows, with the sound of the little creek rippling in his ears, Stanley tried to imagine how a Confederate soldier might have felt.

He couldn't do it.

**Excerpt from *MURDER IN THE MIST***

"I don't think I'm cut out for this," he said. "I feel more foolish than anything."

"You're not giving it a chance," Marilyn told him. "Try to imagine what it would be like to be all alone, separated from your unit. You can hear someone in the woods, but you don't know whether it's someone from your side or from the other. You don't know whether to hide, run, or just stand right where you are."

Stanley closed his eyes and tried to put himself in the place of the soldier Marilyn was describing, but it was no use.

"Maybe I should read *The Red Badge of Courage* again," he said. "Or maybe you should have on the uniform. You're a lot better at this than I am."

"Don't be silly. You'll do just fine."

"Maybe. I wish I was as sure of that as you seem to be."

"You're a trouper, Stanley. You'll get into the part when you have to. Trust me."

"All right. If you say so."

"I say so. You'll be great."

And the funny thing was that she turned out to be right. Stanley did just fine, right up until the minute he got shot.